Best of Southeast Asian Erotica

Best of Southeast Asian Erotica

Edited by Richard Lord

monsoon

monsoonbooks

First published in 2010
by Monsoon Books Pte Ltd
52 Telok Blangah Road, #03–05 Telok Blangah House
Singapore 098829
www.monsoonbooks.com.sg

ISBN: 978-981-08-5436-2

National Library Board, Singapore Cataloguing-in-Publication Data
Best of Southeast Asian erotica / edited by Richard Lord. – Singapore :
Monsoon Books, 2010.
p. cm.
ISBN-13 : 978-981-08-5436-2 (pbk.)

1. Erotic stories, Southeast Asian. 2. Erotic stories, English –
Southeast Asia. 3. Short stories, Southeast Asian. I. Lord, Richard A.
(Richard Alan)

PR9570.S6442
828.995903 -- dc22   OCN650397683

Printed in Singapore

15 14 13 12 11 10   1 2 3 4 5 6

Contents

Introduction

Exploring the Sensual and
The Realm of Possibilities

Just over four years ago, during the Noughties, Monsoon Books elected to take a gamble and bring out a book with the provocative (some might say oxymoronic) title *Best of Singapore Erotica*. The gamble paid off; the book was, at least by the measures of Singapore book sales, a bestseller.

Buoyed by this success, Monsoon has decided to spread its net a little wider and bring out this volume, the *Best of Southeast Asian Erotica*. This time around, there were five countries covered: Indonesia, Malaysia, the Philippines, Thailand, and Singapore once again. As co-editor of the earlier Singapore book and the overall editor of this volume, I admit I was rather curious as to what kind of stories would come our way in this larger scope volume. Two main questions thumped at the back of my head: first, what, if anything, is different about the way erotica is perceived and handled in these five different Southeast Asian lands? And then, would a national character emerge in the submissions we received?

Well, I learned a good deal and was sometimes quite surprised, sometimes confirmed in my expectations as the submissions started flowing in. The large number of submissions we received from Thailand was almost predictable. But the number of captivating submissions from supposedly puritanical Malaysia proved to be our big surprise. Less surprising was the type of stories presented from these two countries.

The Malaysian stories clearly suggested a national character with respect to erotica. For one thing, all of the Malaysian submissions indicate an ironic, sometimes even comic approach to the question of human sexuality. Further, three of the four stories we finally selected reflect an Islamic sensitivity to the subject.

For instance, in the delightful piece that opens this collection, Amir Muhammad presents a comfortably married couple taking a unique approach to reinvigorating their physical intimacy. At the other end of the ethical spectrum, Amirul Ruslan gives us a craven hypocrite, a seemingly devout man who wrestles with his conscience and then discovers his conscience speaks with an all too familiar voice as it calls him back to the straight and narrow.

Another surprise: Thailand's reputation as the capital of the erotic takes a bit of a bruising here. With one exception, the stories from the Land of Smiles all present sexual relationships as something touched with *tristesse*, if not actually wrapped in layers of mutual misuse. While the sex in our Thailand stories is usually hot and easy, the element of love is almost always tainted. This is true even when one of the two main characters whole-heartedly seeks to combine sex with love. The tension between the different types of desire, and their frustration, makes these stories quite compelling.

From the Philippines, we have a trio of engaging stories. Two are by British expat but long-time Manila resident Nigel Hogge, excerpted from two of his novels. Each brings a wry view of the subject and a delightful British sense of humour to the presentation.

But what makes these pieces work so well is the author's clear appreciation of the sexual in brief, chance encounters.

The other Philippine entry, by Annabel Pagunsan, is also excerpted from a novel and presents a newly married couple visiting the groom's extended family back in the Philippines as they are just fitting themselves into their married status. This story is probably more typically Filipino than the other two, and it skillfully delineates the importance of family and social background in relationships.

In *Aphrodite*, the sole Indonesian story we were able to accept, the approach to the subject of sexuality is highly original, elusive even; multi-faceted and presented in a poetic manner, the work invites the reader into a series of different worlds, some gritty and urban, others rural and enchantingly mystical.

Singapore's multicultural nature is amply reflected in the Lion City's contingent of stories: the characters themselves are frequently of mixed heritage while the sexual partners, or the temptations presented, usually cross ethnic and racial lines.

In fact, as in our previous volume of Singapore erotica, the notion of the 'other' (racially or ethnically) frequently spices up the sex in these stories. (In all six Thailand stories, the interracial element is a key component of the erotic enticement.) It is often pointed out that relationships are more open, less insular these days. That would seem to be true across the region. But if these stories are any guide, there is also a lingering sense of taboos, and many of our authors obviously feel that violating these taboos can still play a prime role in stoking the fires of the erotic.

And it's not only ethnic or racial taboos that come into play here: there's also the piquant testing of taboos set to enforce gender identity. In three of the most intriguing stories in the collection, one of the main characters is of ambiguous sexuality, the result of either surgery or nature's whimsy—or both.

But finally, all the stories here celebrate sensuality and sexuality and again proclaim the importance of both in human relationships. Yet each of our authors, and each of the countries represented here, finds a unique way to proclaim this importance.

The sensual and the sexual are indeed realms that leave vast tracts of possibilities still to be explored. The nineteen stories in this anthology explore some of these areas in most commendable ways and they make it clear that erotic literature is indeed an important branch of literature.

Richard Lord
Singapore

MALAYSIA

The Sex Thing
with the Tempoyak

Amir Muhammad

Zeb and Sarah had been having sex for nine and a half months, and she was starting to get bored. It wasn't that she would openly yawn during sex or anything, but she would find her thoughts flying to places other than the man who was actively in bed with her—such as whether she'd remembered to pay the electricity bill, as they were so quick to cut off the supply the last time.

She didn't bring up the topic in case he got offended. Besides, this was an unusually long relationship for her, so she figured that it was inevitable for the initial excitement to fade away after a while. It was probably the natural course of things. Weren't there more important things in a couple's life—mutually enriching adventures that they could embark on together? Maybe they could get season tickets for the Malaysian Philharmonic or something; she'd always vaguely wanted to cultivate an interest in classical music. So she pretended to enjoy the sex and just kept quiet—or rather, just made the unquiet sounds he would expect to hear. After all, she loved him and hoped the feeling was still mutual.

Zeb, however, was fully aware that Sarah was getting bored with him in bed. He noticed it in a certain glaze that came over her eyes, and since they always kept the lights on during sex, he would get to see every little thing in those eyes that he loved so much. He didn't bring up the topic because he didn't want her to get defensive, which might trigger their first fight. It was an unusually long relationship for him, too, but he wanted to make it even longer. So he continued performing his sexual duties the best he could, while thinking of a plan to make things better.

*　*　*

One night in December, he suddenly thought of something. It was an idea that seemed to him quite fine, and so he started grinning. Luckily, Sarah was already asleep by then, so she didn't have to wonder at this sudden, unexplained cheer.

Twenty-four hours later—after they'd both been to work and back separately, as was their usual weekday routine, the only difference being that this time Zeb had made an extra stop along the way home at a dusty bookshop named Toko Junk—they found themselves in bed again.

They were in the middle of foreplay, and without looking up at her face, he could sense (at the most subliminal level) that her enthusiasm was less than his. He suddenly stopped what he was doing. She noticed the change in the usual rhythm and opened her eyes. He was no longer in bed, but standing beside it.

'What's the matter?' she asked, hitching herself up.

'Wait till you see this,' he said, and walked to a large paper bag that he'd left on the dresser. He removed something from the bag and walked back, joining her in bed. She accepted the thing; it was a hardcover book, exquisitely bound in burgundy and obviously old, but written in a script that she didn't understand.

'It's an ancient Javanese sex manual,' he explained.

'It doesn't look Japanese.'

'No, JaVAnese,' he corrected her. 'Luckily, it's a language I can read. It's called the *Serat Centhini* and it's from the early 19th century. It's sometimes referred to as the Southeast Asian *Kama Sutra* because it's so sexually explicit. During the course of the story—and yes, unlike the *Kama Sutra*, there is actually a strong narrative—there are many lessons on how men and women can best pleasure each other, because sexual ecstasy is seen as something that can help people attain spiritual enlightenment.'

'I don't believe you.'

'You can Google it; the book exists!'

'No, I mean I don't believe you can read it. Who on earth reads ancient Javanese?'

'I learned it from my grandfather. Look, I'll prove it to you,' he said, and he lay back against a raised pillow, getting her to do the same against the other one. The pillows, nice and big, were from IKEA.

He put his right arm around her shoulder while his left hand flicked open the musty tome at a random early page. He started reading aloud. The words sounded incantatory, even frightening, as if he were putting a curse on her. She half-expected the room to start filling up with *kemenyan* incense. He read out a whole page, the fingers of his left hand travelling down the book while those of his right hand, almost unconsciously, touched various parts of her. When he was done, he had a slight frown.

'It's very strange,' he said. 'I'm not sure I get it.'

'Why, what is it?' she asked, getting curious in spite of herself.

'It's describing an esoteric sex ritual involving *tempoyak*.'

'*Tempoyak*?'

'Yes, *tempoyak*.'

'I didn't know the ancient Javanese ate fermented durian.'

'This isn't exactly for eating.' And then he described in some detail (he was translating a whole page, after all) how the *tempoyak* should be used. She was incredulous, then amused, then intrigued— but still rather mystified.

'But why would that be pleasurable? It doesn't seem logical,' she said, after the ritual had been described so vividly she felt like a 3-D demonstration had taken place in front of her, like a triple-X version of *Avatar*.

'Don't know. Maybe it was true in the early 19th century but no longer so now.' He wanted to put the book away, but she stopped him. His right hand continued to touch parts of her, and now she placed his left hand, which still held the book, over some other parts of her. As the exquisite burgundy binding of the hardcover travelled over her skin, she thought of the possibilities.

* * *

The next day, as per their usual weekday routine, they took their separate routes to work. She ended up lunching with three of her colleagues at a Malay restaurant. The place was packed, and the whirring fans didn't do much for the humidity, but the food was good. While she had a little *sambal petai* with her rice and *tenggiri* fish, she also asked to take away a Tupperware of *tempoyak*.

'You actually like that stuff? It's so sour,' her colleague Mel said.

'Yeah, I know,' Sarah said, vaguely. She reached for her phone to call Zeb and was dismayed to see that the battery had run out. She could wait to use the charger in the office, of course, but she felt an urgency within her. She asked to borrow Mel's phone.

She dialled Zeb's number from memory, and he took his time answering. Sarah knew she had to keep her part of the conversation discreet because her three colleagues were within hearing distance. She didn't want to seem like some kind of pervert.

'It's me. Borrowed phone. I bought the *tempoyak*,' she said, when he was finally on the other end. 'Should we try the ... recipe tonight?'

He laughed. 'Serious?'

'Yes' she said, keeping her voice light. 'I'm curious to see how it will taste.'

'Okay, but there are a few other items we'll need to get. The tools.'

'Yes, I remember the items. Can we get modern-day equivalents? Some of those ancient ones won't be available now.'

'I will check with IKEA after work,' he said, and she could almost see him wink.

After the call ended, her other colleague, Rini, said, 'Waah, I didn't know you two cooked.'

'There's a first time for everything. It's a Japa— ...

Javanese recipe.'

'Those things tend to be spicy, right?' asked her third colleague, Ling.

'We shall see,' was all Sarah said.

* * *

As promised, he had a bag of IKEA products. They spent a bit of time preparing in the kitchen, and when everything seemed to be in place, he asked, 'Are you ready?' and she replied, 'Sure!'

They did it in the kitchen itself because there were already paper towels and power sockets there. And it was, in a word, awesome. She tingled in places she didn't even know existed; at a precise moment during the ritual, she actually thought her head would swivel around like in a movie possession, because she really felt like she was being taken outside herself, into a more primitive but more vital realm of the senses. Perhaps she was taken out of the Earth into the mythical sky kingdom of Kayangan.

When it was finally over, she wanted to start all over again. He was willing, but there was no *tempoyak* left. When they both stopped panting, he said, 'Tomorrow you can bring a bigger Tupperware.'

That was the start of the most amazing week of her life. She couldn't concentrate at work. The simplest things, such as watching creamer dissolve in coffee, would make her blush with remembered pleasure. It was like everything else became black-and-white while the sex thing with the *tempoyak* every night was not only in colour, but the swirling, explosive palette of a Bollywood musical sequence.

(Why deny it: she'd always preferred Bollywood to classical music. The Malaysian Philharmonic could safely be ignored now.)

She was sure that the sounds they made would sometimes alarm the neighbours, some of whom were terribly nosy, but she didn't care. Couldn't a couple resuscitate Javanese rituals from the early 19th century in the comfort of their own kitchen—or, as was the case, in every other part of their apartment?

Things can't get any better than this, she thought. But she was wrong.

＊　＊　＊

She got back one evening and started undressing immediately. She somehow knew he was in the bedroom. (Since they'd started the sex thing with the *tempoyak*, they had achieved an almost ESP level of communication. They could not only finish each other's sentences but anticipate the other's thoughts. This was probably because the ritual took them into more intimate territory than either had thought possible.)

By the time she got to the bedroom, she was already naked. And he was waiting for her, standing, also wearing only a smile. He didn't have any of the props with him, but even looking at him without the ritualistic paraphernalia—he was just the naked Zeb that she had seen hundreds of times in the past nine and a half months—was enough to get her excited.

She was so happy letting her eyes wander over every inch of him (some inches more than others) that she didn't notice he had his right hand behind his back. Then he brought it out: the book, again.

21

'I've just finished the next page,' he said. 'The page after the description of the sex thing with the *tempoyak*. Would you be interested to try the next level?'

'There is a next level?'

'Yes. The book goes through several stages, each subsequent one meant to bring a couple even closer together in the journey of life.'

She nodded, not daring herself to say anything, not even 'Sure!', even though her mind was filled with exclamation marks.

'Tonight we can go back to basics: just you and me, if that's okay with you. But when you come home tomorrow,' he said, walking towards her, reaching her, doing a few things to her until he brought his lips to her ear and whispered, 'bring a whole durian.'

* * *

A few days later, Zeb was walking along the road that housed the Toko Junk bookshop. The aged proprietor, sitting outside for a respite from the stuffy interior, waved to him and he stopped.

'How are you doing, Mrs Heng?'

'Fine, thank you. Looking for any more books?'

'Not for the moment,' he said cheerfully. 'There are so many I haven't finished yet!'

She watched his retreating back with a smile. If only all customers were like him! He'd sometimes buy things that no one else would buy. Like his most recent purchase: a 19th-century Land Code, a hardcover exquisitely bound in burgundy but written entirely in Hindi. 'Do you read Hindi?' she'd asked.

'No.' She could have sworn he then winked at her. 'But I'll improvise.'

Amir Muhammad is a Malaysian writer, publisher and filmmaker. He has been writing for the print media since the age of 14. Two of his documentaries are banned in Malaysia. His books include *120 Malay Movies* (Matahari Books) and *Rojak* (ZI Publications), both published in 2010. *The Sex Thing with the Tempoyak* was first published in *Rojak* (Petaling Jaya: ZI Publications, 2010).

Aqua-Subculture

Lee Ee Leen

I sold beautiful curiosities in my shop, so it was only fitting that one walked in. However, it was not an antiques shop. My merchandise was a living example of years of human manipulation in enhancing specific genetic traits in fish. I stocked common goldfish, black goldfish supposed to guard the family home from bad *chi*, calicos, neon tetras, comets and bubble-eyed imported specimens. I rented a corner lot squeezed next to a dim sum restaurant in a neighbourhood shopping mall; contrary to what you may have overheard in the management office, my fish did not end up as fillings in the wantons served up for the lunchtime crowd. A week after I had expanded the shop to include marine fish, Andie sauntered through the door.

I tried not to stare at her. Beautiful women are often defensive and accompanied by protective items such as boyfriends and husbands. But she was alone, a towering, slim beauty whose physique almost blended in with the narrow shelves that overlooked the reef tank. With a Harley-Davidson biker's cap tilted over her face, she lured me out from behind the counter.

'How much?' She tapped the glass of the tank to indicate the black-and-white cleaner wrasse, darting around the bigger fish in the tank like harried waiters. For a natural tank janitor and a collector's item, I recommended a cleaner shrimp, a miniature automaton coloured like a barbershop pole and equipped with six jointed legs.

'I am not a beginner,' she stated in a lilting accent that was definitely not local. Her green contact lenses flashed in the fluorescent light. I was naive to think she was referring to her fish-keeping experience.

'Come back in three days. Those wrasse are reserved.' I lied.

Three days later, when I arrived at my shop, she was standing outside the shutter at a quarter to eleven. With those narrow hips wrapped in tight snakeskin jeans, she looked like a boy when viewed from behind. When she turned at the sound of my jangling keys, I saw her breasts constricted under a Boy London T-shirt. 'Please wait outside, miss.'

I learnt her name after I had bagged a cleaner wrasse. The fish flailed as I handed her the plastic bag 'It only has one hour before it suffocates.'

'Kinky,' she muttered as she took the bag. She was not wearing the green contact lenses this morning. I preferred her eyes naturally tawny. She told me her name because she was fed up with my calling her 'Miss' as if I were giving inept instructions to an artillery unit.

'Andie,' she said. 'Like the actress, Andie Macdowell.' She paused and waited for my response, as if I had flubbed a line of dialogue.

'I wasn't named after someone famous.' I told her after some hesitation. I wished I was called Jacques as an alternative to my pedestrian moniker, Jack. When I was young, I saw a documentary on TV about Jacques Cousteau, the French underwater explorer.

But local mispronunciation would flub the Gallic inflection of Jacques, and make it sound more like Jock.

Andie laughed and removed her biker cap. Her black hair fell to the waistband of her jeans. She looked like a mermaid, the black tresses and their green iridescence shimmering above the scaly *faux* snakeskin.

* * *

We met under the fibreglass model of a whale shark in the aquaria in Kuala Lumpur City Centre. I suggested the trip as a natural progression of shared interests. The aquaria were divided into biotopes: coral reef, Amazon River, Malaysian rainforest and mangrove swamp. A tunnel lit by neon-blue track lights connected each biotope.

'Arapaimas mate for life,' I point out to Andie at the Amazon River tank. Two behemoths drift past us in the green water, their bony heads etched with curlicues and ridged scars.

'Fools.' She set her lips together in a compressed line.

'Sea slugs are hermaphrodites—but can't self-fertilize. They still need a partner,' Andie informed me as she pressed her palm on the reinforced glass of the cylinder tank for invertebrates. A specimen unfurled its fuchsia plumes as it clambered over a Venus' Flower Basket, a glassy hollow sponge that imprisons a pair of male and female shrimp for life.

We followed yellow arrows plastered to the wall of the tunnel to the special aquaria exhibit of the month—Australian sea snakes. A large open tank was covered with mesh wire, flanked by signs that unnecessarily warned visitors not to put their hands inside the tank. I peered through the wire and saw two banded sea snakes entwined in a tight double helix, their bodies rippling together in gentle languor. Inspired by this demonstration, Andie slipped her arms around my waist and squeezed until I jerked in pain.

I guided Andie to the shark tank, expecting a little more tenderness from her. A nurse shark burrowed its snout into the sand, scavenging for leftovers. The PA crackled and a voice announced feeding time. Kids rushed to the glass as a diver descended into the tank clutching a wire mesh bag of frozen fish. The diver dealt out the fish like an underwater Jesus feeding the five thousand; the food in the bag did not run out.

Aware of his audience, the diver let his hand linger in the maw of a black-tip reef shark to the shrieks of alarm from the children. Andie smiled at this spectacle, her lips stretched back, revealing teeth that overcrowded her mouth. She was all torpedo sleekness in a grey, sleeveless dress.

We exited the aquaria and flowed into the lunchtime crowd.

Andie stayed in a service apartment opposite KLCC. A basket of fruit on the coffee table enhanced the sparseness of the living room. I noted the absence of an aquarium.

'What did you do with the wrasse?'

'I bought it as a gift.' She waved her hand around as if the question were lingering cigarette smoke and changed the subject. 'Are you hungry?'

We phoned for sushi from a Japanese restaurant near KLCC that provided delivery. Our food would arrive in thirty minutes. Andie selected a pomegranate from the fruit basket. As she started peeling away the skin of the fruit, she told me a story.

A beautiful girl was born to a Thai mother and Swiss father. Her father left not long after she was born. When the girl came of age, she found out that she was different from her friends. She looked like a girl, but was not one on the inside.

'How so?' I asked Andie.

'She can't have children. She has no womb,' Andie replied, and with the sudden shift to present tense, I realized she was talking about herself. Andie had Complete Androgen Insensitivity Syndrome; her body had resisted the development into a male by remaining stubbornly feminine. She was not a transsexual and she hated the term 'intersex'.

'I'm not a freak!' Andie ranted, 'I'm not caught between the two sexes. Males and females are the ones who are strange, because they are the ones who are incomplete. Women are always searching for their other halves and all that magazine bullshit.'

Andie took a deep breath, piled the pomegranate seeds into a glass bowl and joined me on the sofa. She put her head in my lap and asked me to drop the seeds into her mouth. I asked her what I had done to earn this pleasure.

'I just spent a whole afternoon with you,' she smiled up at me. 'And you're the first guy I've met around here who doesn't ask dumb questions about me. You live in the "now". Suppose it comes from watching fish all the time.'

The seeds burst with a tart pop. As the juice spilled, it stained my fingertips scarlet. Like the diver with the shark, I let my fingers remain between her lips for a second too long. She sucked and nipped the pads of my finger, not quite playful. If she drew any of my blood, it mingled with the juice.

Over one of our sushi dinners, I mentioned mating to Andie, about how marine creatures did not go through the awkwardness of sex on dry land. When she had cleared her plate, she went to the bathroom. Andie called for me after ten minutes. I heard the taps running from outside and knocked on the bathroom door.

She poured in the bath salts and the foam and issued me instructions: 'Don't turn around until I say so.'

I heard the taps running, water gushing out. Inspired, I invented a name for a new cocktail: 'Sex in the Bath'. Foam spilled over the rim on the bathtub and drifted over to my bare feet.

'You can look now.'

Andie had skimmed off a layer of thick foam and fashioned a bikini out of it: bubbles shining on her wet skin like sequins sewn onto a body stocking.

The water sloshed around as I climbed inside the tub. I lifted aside a handful of wet hair pressed against her shoulder blades, strands of kelp left on white sand at high tide. The strap of lather on one shoulder had split. I nipped and rasped my teeth along the ridge of a collarbone until I reached the notch at the base of her neck. I dipped my tongue in, the skin tasting salty the same as the mussels at dinner a few hours before. The rest of the makeshift bra had dissolved, exposing her tiny rosewood nipples. My hand reached between her thighs and sought out her niche, fingers discovering that her hole was as shallow as a navel. Andie gasped and shoved me back with the contained violence of a self-defence class. We slid in rhythm against the wall of the tub. Male sea snakes cannot disengage from females until mating is complete.

* * *

My livingroom had a built-in marine aquarium, equipped with backlit glass, harsh and vivid like a screensaver. The cleaner shrimp from my shop were servicing a blue-striped angelfish.

'Humans think they can study animals in tanks and cages, and put them into categories.'

Dressed in a terry-wrap robe, Andie walked over to the window, her profile slashed into shadows by the Venetian blinds. Her rants began like our lovemaking, a sharp tangential stab in a random location, growing in intensity as she located an available target.

I tried to distract her. I pointed to the aquarium. 'Are you talking about my fish?'

'You make them sound like they're your property.'

I went over and put my arms around her to soothe her displeasure.

'You don't own me—I'm not one of the fish in your shop.'

'I have a duty to my shop.'

'Your shop is your property, which has its own set of conditions. She loosed the belt on the robe and opened it before taking my hand and pressing it on her soft breast, 'Duty is unconditional. When you're with me, you are beyond all that.'

'No.' I struggled to deny my body's responses. 'Can we talk about you? Or us??'

Andie rolled her eyes at me and pushed me back towards the sofa. 'Remember the deal, Jack? You don't ask dumb questions about me or anything. We enjoy what we can when we can.'

On the sofa, the bathrobe fell down around Andie as she

climbed above me, a goddess holding up the canopy of the night sky with her body. It was dim under her robe as the moist velvets of our mouths mingled. When she placed her mouth around what she humourously called my 'seahorse', I forgot about duty or business.

*   *   *

Andie was right; my shop was my property and my duty although I had been neglecting it. Dead live food drifted in plastic basins, air pumps broke down and filters clogged up with algae and gave off the metallic tang of nitrates. My courtesy transformed into curtness with customers. As families waited for a table outside the dim sum restaurant, they allowed their children to wander into my shop. I shooed them away with a broomstick, annoyed that these conventional lives and their offspring had intruded into my floating world.

A man entered the shop, tall and white-haired, his skin so tanned that it gave off a violet lustre in the strip lights of the fish tanks. His appearance attested to a life spent under the sun. The juxtaposition was odd; what was his interest in an indoor hobby like aquarium fish-keeping? I realized the connection when he put a plastic bag on the counter; the cleaner wrasse was swimming inside.

'I'm returning the wrasse. My wife told me she bought it from here,' he said with a faint European accent.

I did not answer and tightened my grip on the broom handle. Andie had lied to me about her marital status. Deceived as I was, I had no desire to be killed by a jealous husband.

'Okay, relax.' He held up a gnarled hand to assuage me. 'My

ex-wife. Well, not until she signs the papers. If she signs them.'

I waited for him to get interrogative. Would he ask me to step outside for a fistfight in front of the dim sum restaurant? When I still did not speak, he said, 'Thank you.'

'What for?'

'Andie has no real friends in KL. I suggested a change of scene to her. We even bought a studio apartment in Mont Kiara last year.' He pushed the wrasse towards me. 'Since no one's going to live there now, there's no need to decorate it.'

I opened the till to give him a refund for the fish.

'No, please. I insist.' He refused the money. I asked him what was his job. 'I own a scuba-diving school in Thailand. Hey, maybe you should try it one day.'

I ignored his offer and blurted, 'Do you still have feelings for Andie?'

He smiled as if I had articulated something he could not admit to himself. 'We live apart, but we are not separated. She goes and returns. Nothing's definite with her and that's the deal.'

'I know.' I agreed and thought of the male and female shrimp inside the Venus Flower Basket, an arrangement of complete security but defined by soft translucent bars.

* * *

Andie sent a blank email with a photo attachment to my business mail address; a fussy snapshot of sea snakes mating, taken with an underwater camera. I replied with a brief thank you and never heard from her again.

My customers thought I had closed my shop for a month. Instead, I renovated it and got rid of the marine fish and invertebrate tanks. I applied for a license to sell dogs and cats. The shop was noisier with barks and meows, but at least it distracted me from thinking about Andie. My new employees did not understand why I was obsessed with checking the sex of new puppies and kittens. I was looking for recurrences of Andie's condition in nature.

Of course, I never found any, but conventional family life found me when a petite woman walked into my shop one evening, tearful that her boyfriend had stood her up outside the dim sum restaurant.

However, my fiancé baulked at making love in the bathtub. She told me I could get hurt. She did not understand when I replied that I had already been hurt that way.

Lee Ee Leen was born in London, UK. She has an MA in English from Royal Holloway College, University of London. In 2009 she was shortlisted for MPH Alliance Bank National Short Story Award and she has reviewed films for *The Directory of World Cinema: American Independent* (Bristol: Intellect Books, 2010).

The Politician

Amirul B Ruslan

Everything had to be discreet. This was the seventh time he had done this, but each time he still felt the usual pangs of worry, of guilt. Voices played out in his head. One of them was the monotone of a newsreader as she—he always envisioned it as a she, and so it must be a she—presented the lurid details of this scandal. One of them was the cruel chastising by his late mother, a voice gone from this earth over twenty years, but constantly returning to haunt his subconscious each time he performed this deviant act.

The hotel he was now staying in on the blissful, blisteringly hot island of Penang was a colonial relic. His father wouldn't have approved. His father hated all things colonial, and indeed gave up his life fighting colonial oppressors. First the Japanese, then the British. He fought proudly to Independence and marched into— no, the politician thought, no. He cut the thought there and then, questioning, pleading to his mind: Why do I have to reminisce on my father's achievements now? Was it because he was a religious man? Was it because if he knew, he would call me a deviant, a pervert?

The hotel was grand and almost over-the-top in its pretension. Whatever British elegance it had in the 1920s when it was built was now hidden behind layers of coarse Malaysian 'aesthetic' of out-of-place Ionic pillars, tiled floors and wide, gold-painted door frames. The politician had been an architect before he became a politician, and even after decades of being in the country's less-than-refined body politic, this vulgar so-called sophistication wounded his senses.

But what mattered most was not the furniture or the windows or the high ceilings or the grand piano in the lobby or the way the staff—Malays no less, good Malays playing submissive servants to the under-dressed hedonist tourist masses that flocked to this island paradise—shuffled around. What mattered most was that everything today stayed discreet. And as he walked along the corridor leading to the hotel lounge, brushing away an overeager bellboy asking, 'Y.B., anything I can help you with?' with that subservient tone in Malay, he saw her.

She was standing by the reception, looking busy. She had her BlackBerry out, and while it seemed like she was furiously tapping out a message, some important email, no doubt, the politician knew that she was paying attention to the lounge with her darting eyes. When their eyes met from across the hall, she pocketed her BlackBerry and gave a small nod. That was all. A small nod.

She looked good, just as she always did, this thirty-five-year-old woman who had been sneaking away to rendezvous with him for over four years now. She was a whore—he couldn't bear calling her profession by any other name, as they all felt overly sanitized. Prostitute? Escort? Call girl? Courtesan? *Don't kid yourself, Y.B., she's a whore, pure and simple.* But she was a whore he felt a great deal of attachment to, and he treated these trysts with a great deal of excitement.

He met her at the elevator. He was already inside, the only person in there, when she rushed towards the closing doors. As if to show his potent chivalry, instead of pressing down on the Open button, he instead lodged himself into the doorway, letting her pass. Cunningly, he also sneaked a grope in as she squeezed past, one hand reaching out to feel the fine curvature of her ass. She didn't seem to like it. He did.

His room was on the seventeenth floor, a luxurious suite that was overly indulgent, even to him, for someone who was only going to be staying on the island for one night. The elevator lurched upward. He idly whistled. She smoothed her blouse. She was standing at the corner, almost vulnerable as she seemed to hide away. A poster partitioned away by a cold glass pane sat beside her, promoting the latest Filipino house band that was playing at the hotel. He opened his mouth, and tilted closer to her. Fifth floor. 'Dahlia …' he began.

She didn't even seem to pay any attention.

Sixth floor. He inched closer again, small inches growing to bigger inches. He cornered her where she was. She looked up at him. Finally, some eye contact. His hand tried for her thigh, the one wrapped in the fine black stocking under her skirt. He half-expected her to slap him. She didn't. Her furious, cold stare still kept his gaze, as his fingers brushed up. Eighth floor. Her skirt lifted just a bit …

Then she commanded him. 'Step away right now.' She spoke with such strength in her voice. Domination. He instinctively followed as she instructed. He moved back to his corner. Ninth floor. She turned to face him, brushing her skirt back to its previous meticulous, flawless state. Her voice softened, but there was no mistaking the vigor still within. 'Are you stupid? There's a camera right there, up above where you're standing.'

So there was. It wasn't like he didn't know that; of course he knew. He just couldn't resist. He couldn't resist being told off, being called stupid, the sort of verbal abuse he could only find from her, or in Parliament.

'For someone who makes such a big deal about discretion ...' she trailed off, as if uninterested in continuing in that thread. The politician looked up at the ceiling, a smooth surface refashioned as a mirror. He saw the top of her head, the push of her bounteous breasts. It was like topography to him. A silence held. Thirteenth floor. He didn't want to succumb to apologizing. He knew he would be doing a lot of that later, in the room.

Seventeenth floor. When the elevator doors opened, he stepped out with confident strides left, towards his suite. He shuffled through his coat pockets to find the keycard. Room 1726, there. A cleaning lady, Malay again, another deferential Malay with incessant bowing, stepped away as he passed, muttering, 'Good evening, Datuk Haji.' The last honorific was particularly ironic. They called him a Haji as if he were truly the religious man he appeared, even as he used their facilities for illicit pleasures.

He reached his door and craned his neck to see the corridor as he grasped the handle and slid the keycard in. His whore had not followed him yet. She was professional like that. His room, when he entered, was spotless. The large bed had been done, probably less than ten minutes ago, and he stepped to the bathroom. Both the suite and bathroom doors were left slightly ajar, to invite his guest in to join him.

In the bathroom, he felt another sudden pang of worry: it was because he saw his reflection. But with the light off there, he first saw a different figure. He saw his father, the real Datuk Haji, a political heavyweight who was as much the Malay warrior before Independence as afterwards. He saw his father frown at him, liquid disapproval causing him a near panic attack. When his clammy hands reached for the light switch and the room bathed him in light and warmth, the reflection melted into the somewhat more comforting sight of his own face.

He heard the door swing gently open as he washed his hands, staring at himself. He looked like a true Captain of Industry. At nearly fifty, he was still in perfect health, with a body that was more accurately described as 'sturdy'. His features were solid, and in their own way, handsome. His beard was trimmed just enough, a calculated move to make him appear vaguely religious while unquestionably professional. He had a lot of hair still, in contrast to most of his party's leaders.

He wiped his face with wet hands. He looked a lot like his father, except for missing the warrior's icy eyes, the permanent disapproving frown. Again he dispelled the thought as he loosened his tie, hung his coat on the rack, and kicked his shoes off. He stepped towards the bed. Dahlia was already there, waiting for him.

The whore wore a grey skirt from some famous Italian brand that ended sharply at her knees, and her blouse was white and immaculate. She had glossy black high heels that highlighted her beautifully shaped feet, and black stockings like a fabric version of his yellow brick road. To top it off, she wore glasses that magnified the fortitude in her eyes. He sat down beside her.

She looked at him wordlessly, and rotated ever so slightly, one hand placed down between them and balancing her and she placed her right leg on his lap. Her foot fidgeted, and he removed her shoe. 'No,' she said, in English, always English, even though English was his much weaker language, 'Put it back on, and do it again.'

There was a strict precision to this process, and she didn't let him deviate from it in any way. He rubbed his thumb against her ankle as he slipped her black heel off. He must have done it correctly, as he was rewarded with her kissing down on his clothed shoulder, feeling her hot breath over his shirt. She withdrew her right leg and proffered her left, one hand tracing over the politician's back. Her fingernails pressed against the fabric of his shirt. She continued kissing. He continued removing her shoe.

Every act she chose to do was a carefully calculated step in her flawless seduction. Were the politician a more worldly man, he would have compared her grace to a geisha's. He kissed her toe and received a sharp knock to the back of his neck from her wrist in return. He looked at her, bewildered. 'Not yet,' she said, glaring. The good whore giveth and the good whore taketh away: she slid both legs away from him, and no longer kissed his shoulder.

'*Maaf*,' he apologized quickly. In public he was a man of very few apologies. A scandal in Parliament two terms ago as a result of a remark deemed racist had effectively cost him a minister's post. It wasn't racist, it was a fact of life, he reasoned. A man must speak with conviction, and never back down. That last saying was his father's ... again. *God, why did he have to come down from Heaven to advise me now?* he thought, returning his attention to Dahlia.

She had taken to the far end of the bed, propping pillows to support her back. She spread her covered legs but pushed down on the middle edge of her skirt, limiting what he could see. 'For a whore, you are really ...' But that was the best his English could say. His words faded away. She paid those words no mind.

Still pressing down the hem of her skirt as she spread, a twinkle in her eye, a rare approving one, invited him to come get her. 'Unbutton my blouse,' she commanded again. He positioned himself between her legs and leaned forward. It was timid, careful. He started with the top; she only ever let him start with the top. The politician's fingers no longer had the dexterity of his sketching days, and they groped for the button. He released each button with the sort of precision he knew she wanted, and then with each, she sighed a little. These micro-moans were so soft it seemed as if it were only for her own ears. He was three buttons down when he felt Dahlia's hands wrapping his neck. She felt his neck, and with thumbs she began to choke him.

He finished unbuttoning, having tugged out the tucked-in portion of her blouse, and now her blouse was no longer tight and precise, but dangling out, releasing those breasts. He thought in Malay, and then in English, that there was no truly accurate word for them in both languages. They were not just breasts, they were more than that. Bosom was too formal. Tits was the closest that he could think of, but that word was too dirty and American, and not a word he would ever think of using.

'What are you thinking?'

He looked up at her, wrenched away from that distraction. 'Nothing,' he assured her.

'You never think.' It was the end of the conversation already.

She had incredible power in her words; no party leader had that sort of authority. The Prime Minister, all the Prime Ministers in the past, none of them could match up to her sovereign vocal will. The word he thought of, for some reason, was *supremasi*. Supremacy?

Next she placed both feet on his chest, blocking him. He rubbed the back of her thighs with his hands, feeling light sweat on her skin. He leaned closer but she pushed him back, still. She made a minor striptease as she removed her stockings. Each move was elegant as she writhed to free herself. Her feet dropped, toes catching onto the band on his pants, and with adroitness he had never seen before, even from her, she was able to unzip his pants, her feet doing all the work for him. Her hands moved behind her and slipped under her blouse. She undid her bra, an elegant French piece with laces and frills she wouldn't let him see or touch, and it slipped right off, falling forward.

The politician looked at his Rolex, but that moment of inattention earned him a brief kick to his chin. He apologized again. 'Kiss my feet,' she said, speaking seductively, brushing her feet up against the politician's face. He did as she said. It was a strange feeling for him to be treated like this, to be instructed. He kissed up from her legs, up, up, until reaching her moist inner thighs, sweat-slicked, perspiration the only reminder that she was as mortal as he was. As beholden to urges as he was.

He waited for her to instruct him to pleasure her, but she never did. Without this permission, he seemed to be unable to kiss further, tentatively rubbing where he couldn't kiss with a thumb. He could smell her, now. She wore dark grey nylon panties similarly laced and frilled as her bra. She still remained stoic and silent.

'I want to— ' he attempted, before she shot him down with a glare. He kept that gaze for a while, before she prodded him with a foot down against his groin. She probably wanted him to continue, but not progress further. This teasing was just like her.

This went on for another ten minutes. Up and down, up, slightly, then down, slightly, tracing this invisible iron curtain. He knew she liked it, because he could smell her getting heavier with lust, a stronger, more potent, physical scent. At one point, licking her thigh, he even tasted something different, other than the taste of moist flesh and salty sweat. Earthier, more real. Surely it would not be long, the politician thought.

Eventually she relented, two fingers moving the panties aside. He stretched forward, an instinctive motion. He somehow could sense his late father chiding him, though this time not because he was some deviant adulterer, but instead because he was now this servile, obsequious pathetic creature made to follow specific instructions from this whore.

But ayah, he thought, *she is not just any woman!* She could control anybody if she wanted to. His father shot back an angry, otherworldly retort: *Be a man and take what you want, when you want it. When you grovel, you bring disgrace to your so-called achievements, you bring disgrace to your role as a leader of men, head of your family.*

He lapped her up when she unthinkingly allowed him, with no other desire than to give her pleasure. He was not actually there; he was arguing with ghosts. If he were there, he would have heard Dahlia's moans, first starting short and small, and then growing in volume.

His face was full of it, all in it. He faced his father and asked aloud, antagonized, 'What do you want from me?'

'More,' he heard a confident, salacious response, but it came from Dahlia, not his father. This brought him back to where he was. No ghosts were here.

He pulled back, wiping his face. He simply could not go on. Dahlia didn't look like her usual self anymore, suddenly. She no longer looked flawless and professional. Her hair was slightly untidy, and she was blushing, and she bit her lip and looked ... different. She was partially undressed, and so was he. He looked around and no ghosts were here.

He reeled back in horror. 'Go, just ... go.'

'What?'

'Please, go,' he pleaded. He took his wallet out of his pants pocket and pulled out crisp notes. Fifty ringgit. A hundred. Another hundred. Two, three, five, eight hundred. He flicked them her way.

This broke her icy coolness. She was confused, but so was he. 'You haven't even ...' she stuttered.

'I don't want to.'

A long moment passed, tense between them. She collected the notes from the bed, repositioned her panties. She took her bra and didn't even ask him for help putting it back on. He just stared at her. She put her shoes back on and walked over to the door. She gave him one last look, and this time he saw some strange vein of pity in there. Pity for who, for him?

When she left, he exhaled. He stared to the ceiling as he lay down in bed. Her scent was strong, and her lasting presence was damp on the covers. As he stared up, he tried to conjure those ghosts, begging for their approval, that now she was out of the way, they could talk. But no ghosts were here.

No ghosts were here.

Unlike the politician in *The Politician*, Amirul B Ruslan is a twenty-year-old Malaysian journalist and writer. His journalism work has been published in *TELL* magazine and *The Star*. *The Best of Southeast Asian Erotica* is his fiction debut.

Awakening

Yusuf Martin

Syafiqah was not sure just where the old fragment of book came from, but she was bored and it was the only material to hand that she had not read. She had finished the American book about the teenage vampire, the slushy one that was made into a film, that one with that American girl whose father had been a mediocre country and western singer some years before. Therefore, as it was raining, she reached for the yellowing book, wiped the dust carefully from the first and last pages and the broken spine, sat on the corner of her bed and began to read.

In the golden morning kampong half-light, still slightly scented by a smoky mosquito coil, Amir Hussain, a bronzed, muscular young Indian stood in his newly laundered white dhoti, which lingered teasingly between the girlish curvature of his waist to a centimetre above his youthful knees.

Syafiqah noted that the book had no actual cover, only pages and a spine. Several of the first stories, in what appeared to be a volume of short stories, seemed to be missing. All the information Syafiqah had about the book was in fine print at the top of the page facing her—page 62. This suggested that the book, when it was whole, had been *The Best of Southeast Asian Erotica Volume 2*, whatever that was.

She shrugged; the title meant nothing to her, but, a little intrigued, she began dipping into the story. At sixteen, with all the normal peculiarities of a mid-teen, Syafiqah readily found herself identifying with the main character, Farah, a Malay girl who, like Syafiqah, lived in a small rural kampong.

Eagerly, Syafiqah read on, but a little puzzled.

Shafts of Mediterranean yellow light pierced the musky ambience of the wooden lean-to's interior. It revealed a fresh glistening moistness on Amir's arms and upper torso as he strained to manipulate firmly resistant oiled dough, in preparation for making roti canai.

'Shafts of Mediterranean'. Syafiqah had read about the Mediterranean. It was in Europe, wasn't it? Why were there shafts of European light coming into a kampong lean-to. Was it a kampong lean-to in Europe then? How odd.

With a combination of curiosity and the need to be engaged in something, Syafiqah decided that to enjoy the story, she must really put her questioning aside until she had finished reading it, otherwise there was no way she was going to enjoy it. So, on she read ...

Small beads of sweat gathered at his brow, catching the sunlight as Amir toiled in the warmth of his father's morning shop, serving to highlight the smooth, rich, dark, chocolate brownness of his skin. Carefully, he wiped the salty, oily sweat away, preventing it from falling into the dough he was kneading and tainting it.

'Eee—yuk, sweat,' said Syafiqah with a mock shudder, then 'Mmm ... chocolate.'

Amir was customarily focussed, earnest about his task as he continued massaging the moist dough until it became pliant, kneading the soft, slightly resistant substance, feeling it, in its tenaciousness, bouncing back at the touch of his firm masculine hands. For a moment, just for a moment, the soft silky dough enveloped his hands in a supple oily caress. Busy, Amir did not allow the dough to linger, rejecting its touch and the promise of soft intimacy.

Ten-what? What is tenaciousness, is it like nine-aciousness, but with one extra. Syafiqah reached for her *Oxford Advanced Learner's Dictionary* and looked the word up. Ah, yes, okay. Well, why couldn't they say that then? she said to herself, frowned and once more began to read.

In the robust rhythm of his work method, Amir could feel the smooth slippery dough squeeze between his strong fingers like a gentle lover's kiss, warm, soft yet irrepressibly elusive. Repeatedly, Amir touched the waiting dough, and the dough, though to all intents and purposes inanimate, touched him gently, lovingly back. Even when Amir was a little rough, the dough embraced his roughness, subsumed it into itself and gave pliancy in return, understanding that tough love often came before the needed tenderness.

When the initial pulling and touching were spent, when Amir understood that the dough, despite qualms, was truly ready, Amir would take firm hold of the oiled, manipulated dough in both of his strong, damp hands, lift the dough and toss it back firmly, almost roughly onto its oiled bed. He stretched the dough, massaged it, feeling it relax, become more submissively elastic under his sturdy, determined hands. Again, the supple dough would be lifted and

47

thrust back, down onto the waiting surface, and again, and again, adding to its already acquiescent suppleness. A total of eight times, the now obedient dough would be lifted and returned, forcefully, manfully to the oily surface, its compliance subtly growing with each vigorous stretch.

Quickly, the dexterous Amir would flip the corners of the oily dough over, side by damp side and side over oily side into the centre, until all four sides of the griddle bread lay together at the centre of the dough, forming closely intimate layers. Then, the mass would be lifted once more and, deftly grabbing one side, Amir would gently pull it over the whole—a headscarf over a newly married woman's wanton tresses, indicating her freshly found sensual status, binding the succulent, moistly accommodating layers together.

These infinitely smooth layers of kneaded dough and oil would aid the bread to become crispy, comfortably hard when heated on the sturdy flat griddle, separating them out, giving the roti canai its traditional crusty layered texture and deeply delicious flavour. Amir would manhandle each roti canai in exactly the same way, resolutely stretching and pulling, grasping and caressing until the whole batch was ready for the griddle and, ultimately, the ecstasy of gratuitous consumption by some waiting, welcoming, mouth.

Mmm, this is making me hungry; I wonder what *Mak* is making for lunch. Syafiqah tried to ignore her growing hunger pangs and returned to the text.

Most days, in the glow of the early morning and in the failing roseate light of evening time, Amir worked hard for his father— making roti canai at their rural wooden lean-to and making money by selling the crispy, slightly oily, unleavened griddled breads to their eager regular customers.

Through his ardent toil, Amir gained in stature both in his family and in the local community. The heroic Amir's hard working diligence was the talk of the kampong. He was regular, punctual, and served the best-made roti canai for miles around. Everyone knew this, everyone appreciated this.

For the few idle female customers—those with nothing better to do than to dream, sigh over young athletic men—and the few heavily breathing male customers too, it also helped that Amir was devilishly handsome, with sharp, aesthetically pleasing Indian features. For he was as close as the kampong dwellers would ever get to the uncommon beauty of an Indian movie star. No doubt, Amir being comely added more than a frisson of spice to the kampong dwellers daily lives and to their purchasing of the layered breads, knowing that, inevitably, Amir was there waiting, silently servile to service their pleasure.

Because of Amir's youth, his gentle, yet firm mannerisms and his obvious beauty, he seemed to attract many admirers, young and old. Early in the morning, every morning, as the kampong awakened from another hot, sultry night of insect orchestrations and firefly illuminations, before too many other kampong dwellers were abroad, two mid-teen schoolgirls—Farah and Mira—would be sent by their mothers to collect roti canai for their respective father's breakfasts. It had become their daily routine.

Along the worn kampong track, between the roundly, curvaceously pendulous papaya and the firmly erect banana plants, past shadowy tall coconut trees blessed with hirsute rotund fruit and scented curry-leaf bushes, the two friends would walk, perhaps a little too eagerly, heading in the scant morning light towards the wooden lean-to where Amir, the kampong's master baker, created roti canai.

A short time ago, shortly after Hussain's son Amir had taken over the making of the much desired roti canai from his father, the two girls had discovered, quite by accident, a loose board at the rear of the lean-to where Amir wrestled with dough. At first, the loose board, hanging limp and uninteresting, held no interest to the two girls, but when Farah, the slightly elder of the two, approached the misplaced plank, it seemed somehow more erect. She managed to peer through the gap its displacement had made, and practically melted at the sight of the golden Amir as morning shafts of sunlight played across his hard-working form.

Hastily, guiltily, Farah wanted to replace the board. She blushed. She momentarily had been tempted to keep the discovery to herself; however, at Mira's insistence, she let her friend gaze through the hole—into wonderland.

That adrenalin-pumping, pubescent hormones-raging morning, the two girls, now more than a little excited, giggled all the way back home and, later, giggled all the way to school on the banana-coloured bus. At school, they kept their warm, dark secret until it was time to catch the ancient yellow bus back home once more, then giggled and fantasised all the way back to their homes.

It was at that point that there was a knock on the door. '*Adik*, what are you doing in there? You are so quiet.' Self-consciously, Syafiqah dropped the book fragment to the floor, giving it a little kick so it slid under her bed—she was worried that her mother might catch her reading unsuitable material. 'Nothing

Mak, just tidying.'

'Okay. Don't forget that I will need help with the laundry later.'

'No, *Mak*,' said Syafiqah. Her mother had not entered Syafiqah's bedroom, so, when she considered it safe again, Syafiqah got down on her hands and knees and dragged the tomb out from where it rested—under the bed amongst dust and black-and-white house lizard debris. With a tinge of excitement now, she began to read on.

The following day, each girl dared the other to spy through the gap in the wooden boards, but neither dared to as they were frightened that they would be caught—and what could they possibly say in their defence, if they were caught. Their secret remained between them, as tangible as the breasts that began to strain their blouses.

Some days and some warm, dream-filled nights went past, with the longing to spy on Amir becoming greater with each passing day, until Farah, untypically alone, stopped while walking to the lean-to for her father's breakfast.

Carefully, she walked to the back of the wooden lean-to and, looking around to make certain she was not being observed, prised open the already loose board. The gap was ever so slight, but large enough for Farah to see what she desired to see. Cautiously, guiltily, she put her almond eye right up against the opened crack, and gazed into the musty depths of the wooden lean-to.

The beautiful young Amir, with his back to the intently spying girl, was intent upon kneading the soft dough for roti canai. Farah, dressed for school in her light blue-and-white uniform and carrying the payment for her father's roti canai in her hand, had crept to the rear of the lean-to as carefully as she could, so as not to make a sound. She had prised open the hanging loose plank, making a gap between the wooden boards. Wary not to mark her school clothes, Farah had pulled over a discarded piece of paper to kneel on and gleefully nestled down to, once again, watch Amir.

Surreptitiously, enthusiastically, Farah observed the sweet morning light as it playfully kissed Amir's toned body, lightly caressing him and alternately revealing his skin—golden in the morning shafts of light, then warm chocolate as he moved slightly into shadow. Amir stirred, pulling and pushing at his bread, his hard shiny muscles flexing and relaxing as he energetically twisted the dough before him.

Good grief, said Syafiqah to herself ... and continued.

Next door, but a fluttering heartbeat or two away, the kampong corner shop was beginning to stir. The gnarled, ancient owner could be heard treading the wooden floorboards, almost dragging his slippered feet with his aged step, then unlatching the shop door from the inside, there was a sharp 'clink' as the rusted metal arm hit the top of the protective metal sleeve and 'clunk', as it fell.

Frozen with anticipation, Farah could hear the store owner moving back inside his shop, heading towards the now whistling kettle blowing its head of steam into the waiting morning. He needed to tend to the preparations for his customers' morning tea, as soon, if Farah dallied too long, the shop owner's customers would be milling around inside and outside of the kopi shop, too close to where she knelt for her comfort ... and her reputation.

Sleek Amir breathed a little more deeply at his work. Flexing his slender, toned arm muscles, Amir plunged his strong brown hands deep into the resisting dough, pulling and stretching at the dough for as hard and as long as he could last.

Without pause, he pummelled the dough with practised, energetic fists, elbowing the dough with swift strong motions, twisting and manipulating the dough until, eventually, he was forced, momentarily, to stop, to take breath, glowing like a wrestler, sweat running in tiny rivulets down his smooth back.

Turning on the electric fan for a little air, Syafiqah eagerly read on.

Amir straightened to ease his back muscles. Suddenly, he thrust his head back, tensing, then releasing, tensing, then releasing the taut muscles at the back of his neck. Just for a second, Farah fantasised about Amir's head movement, imagining it as mimicking that of an Indian starlet's as she whipped her wet black hair back in an arc, the slight sweat in Amir's hair resembling water spraying in some passionate, romantic South Indian film, to the weighty rhythm of a Tamil music director. Amir's neatly cropped hair, however, was not the luscious tresses of a film starlet. But to Farah's eyes, his gesture echoed the sheer poetry of the filmi moment perfectly.

Next, putting his hands on the top of his dhoti at his waist, thumbs to the rear while his fingers faced forward, Amir leaned backward and pushed gently but firmly against his back muscles, then repeated the same exercise forward, then to the right, and to the left, stretching and easing his muscles as he did so. There was a feline grace and choreography to his movements, and somewhere, deep inside, he was no longer Amir, son of Hussain, maker of roti canai, but the sprightly satyr Prabhu Deva dancing to the lyrical strains of 'Urvasi Urvasi' by the maestro A. R. Rahman.

Prabhu Deva? Ah yes, *Mak* used to like him, but Michael

Jackson was better. Syafiqah continued reading.

Witnessing the beauty and grace of the young Amir's movements, breathing in achingly short gasps, Farah's budding teen chest rose and fell in helpless excitement. She pressed her young soft hand against her moist mouth, tasting the saltiness of her fingers as she tried to stifle her little involuntary cries, terrified lest the object of her awe hear her. Farah, inextricably caught between the wantonness of her nascent desire and her very real need for caution, found that she was unable to tear her eyes away from the movements of the exquisite Indian.

Guiltily, Syafiqah turned towards the door, checking to see that she had bolted it. She was excited, but a little wary too, lest her mother see what she was reading. Syafiqah had the distinct feeling that her mother would not approve. She turned her eyes back to the page she was reading.

The mesmerised girl watched the delicious boy as xanthous yellow light played across his graceful, sensuous, moving body. Pressing her eager eye against the hole made in the wood, as silently as she was able, Farah observed as Amir fluidly glided to music of sensuous beats obviously sounding only in his own head. Farah, if she had not been delectably awestruck before, was now as her eyes drank in Amir's all but silent dance performance.

Ignoring the fact that 'xanthous' was not in her English dictionary, Syafiqah skipped over the word intending to look it up on the Internet, at school. She did not want to stop the flow of her reading worrying about strange, exotic-sounding words.

The minute sounds of Amir's naked feet on the floor, a gentle whoosh of air as his arm swept, in waves, in circles, was all the accompaniment there was to his satyr dance, and all Farah needed to be caught by his beauty and style. For those few minutes, she was in the thrall of glamour, beguiled by the Indian, fascinated by him.

Farah did not understand her feeling of longing. It had never been a part of her repertoire of feelings; until now. After sixteen and a half years, her body had reached puberty (and beyond) almost before she had realized what was taking place. It was only the obvious tell-tale signs of needing to wear a towel at certain times of the month, a little extra down in personal, private places, and the blossoming of her breasts which alerted her to her changing status.

Now, noting Amir's silent dance, Farah felt warmth expanding inside her, changing her, perhaps forever. It was only while looking at this young Indian that Farah had any inkling of the woman she may yet become, sometime in her future.

If it had not been so embarrassing, the sudden warmth she experienced between her thighs and the unexpected tightening of her chest beneath her school uniform might have overwhelmed her as she watched the perfection of Amir's silent dance.

As it was, her cheeks coloured with a blush, she felt her face become heated. Slowly, Farah tentatively put one hand beneath her school uniform to see if she bled; she did not. The sudden warmth was not that of her monthlies, so her fingers came away clear ... but sticky, as she involuntarily sighed a world- changing sigh, tingling a little with a small tremor of aftershock.

Syafiqah stared at the book page, and then read the paragraph over again. 'Coo,' she said quietly to herself. Then she read it for a third time, just in case she had misread it the other two times. 'Phew,' she said as she read on.

To Farah, her sensations were not at all unpleasant, just inexplicable. She had neither the words nor the experience to describe what she was beginning to feel. She was certain that she no longer felt like the child she had been, but something else. Farah watched, and as she watched, she grew. As she watched, she gasped, a soft almost sensual gasp, a pretty gasp entirely suited to her young, inexperienced years.

It was a sharp intake of breath, a brief moment of inhalation, which in itself was paltry but summed up all her feelings and sensations at that very moment in time. That gasp reflected Farah's myriad of feelings, thoughts, sensations, all new, all unnamed, awaiting her recognition. The gasp was the recognition.

Syafiqah stared at the book. Her heart was racing; she was scared and excited, scared to be caught reading such material, but also more than a little excited by the words. Once more, she checked the door, then turned to her bedroom window and made sure that the curtains were closed. With her heart sounding in her ear, she read more.

Catching his breath from his labours, Amir patted the dough with hands shining like gold in the lean-to's brightening light. Then, when he was ready, he turned towards the rear of the shack and smiled a broad smile right to the spot where Farah was watching.

Farah, shocked, embarrassed, but with a small charge of excited electricity shooting through her body, shyly moved back from her spy-hole. As she did so, she stumbled and fell. Farah's careless tumble caused the loose plank to fall, and the one next to it also. Ungracefully, Farah tumbled into the half-light of the wooden lean-to, her skirt in distinct disarray, revealing the curvature of her calves. A breathless, panting Farah landed almost at Amir's feet. To him, as he gazed at her, it was as if Aishwayra Rai herself had tumbled magically into his domain. Smiling, the glistening Amir reached a hand down to her ...

That was it.

As Syafiqah read, she noticed that the page opposite the one she was on had been torn out. The numbering jumped from page 82, the page she was on, to page 85. It was obvious to her that the story ended somewhere between those pages, and there was more than a little disappointment showing in her face with this momentous realisation. With some annoyance, Syafiqah sellotaped the yellowing fragment of book to the base of her bottom drawer in her chest of drawers, believing it to be safe there.

Later, as Syafiqah was at the back of the kitchen, helping her mother place the pinching pegs out onto the rinsed washing, on their makeshift washing line, she turned to the older woman.

'*Mak*,'

'Yes *Adik*,'

'Where can I get a copy of an old book?'

Yusuf Martin was born in London. He has a first degree in Philosophy, two master's degrees in Art and is a qualified graphic designer and social worker. Yusuf is a freelance writer for magazines and newspapers. He has had stories published by Silverfish Books, MPH and Matahari Books in Malaysia.

INDONESIA

Aphrodite

Suzanna Kusuma

Scene 1: Sunset

Under corrugated roofs, silky bed sheets, her whispers and sounds are carried off in the hiss of traffic from nightfall towards dawn. Sun falls.

With it, streaks of fog lurk and hover over quiet alleyways. Mice skitter around plundering morsels of leftovers. The wasted moon overlooks. A drooping silent witness to the frolics ... A watchful tower to the jealousies and rivalries spurred by her whimsical gestures that entice and provoke men who find in her both the goddess they worship and the witch they would torture and kill.

Kali Jodoh is rows of unlicensed shag houses along the heavily polluted Ciliwung River, somewhere in West Jakarta district. The river stench mingled with cheap alcohol lures bystanders and travellers alike. Curiously drawn to the bright yellow spots of kerosene lamps burning through gaps of asymmetrical doors (invitingly loose and fragile), motorcyclists buzz in and out of the alleyways while quietly picking up and dropping off passengers. Further into the alley, in some hidden nooks and corners, are glimpsed silhouettes of luxury cars which at the sign of dawn would swerve quietly away, leaving their spots empty for food peddlers. It is also not uncommon to find police cars among these luxury cars.

The dense flow and murmur of old Ciliwung River permeates the night. And as the moon wanes, the inhabitants of *Kali Jodoh* ready themselves for the judgment of daylight bursting through.

Scene 2: Domesticated

At night, he seeks the woman who tantalizes his cock with her tongue. He likes to fix his gaze to the clouds as she makes her way up and down, up and down. He had come thrice inside her mouth that day.

His children call him 'daddy' the way Americans do to sweet, doting fathers. He bought them a puppy one occasion-less day, despite his wife's disapproval of pets. They named the puppy Bruno. He convinced his wife children should learn the blessings of having other living creatures to add on to the joy of living.

The same night, he made love to his wife and unselfishly took his time waiting for her orgasm while all along reliving the memories of the tongue teasing, and teasing, and teasing. His explosions rapidly approach as her swift, unyielding embrace commands. He has nowhere to go, nowhere to be, but inside her.

Scene 3: Conquest

Soft undulations of mountains and valleys he caresses with his bare hands every day. His eyes are not as privileged as his hands—though you can argue such is his privilege. More importantly, however, is his gift of subtlety. He is quite used to women who are liars—when asked if they are comfortable, they say, 'Oh yes, perfectly', with their arms and legs pressed tightly on the side as though they were fitting into a tube. He would then cover them over with a piece of silk and let the slippery flow of the fabric persuade them to be just as airy and slacken their rigid pose. Soft feather works beautifully, too, for the more glamorous sort who are not ticklish and enjoy the voluptuous teasing.

He communicates mainly by touching. While his fingers massage, he listens to the skin as it contracts ... softens ... relaxes ... opens ... widens ... quivers ... twitches ... jerks ... and he responds to them appropriately, as attentive lover- devotees do. The shyest and most rigid in turn relinquish their defensive armor: unhook their bras, wiggle down their panties, untie their hair knot. Not surprisingly, they feel liberated in consequence.

Lying naked on the futon, his blindness emboldens them temporarily before they re-emerge in the outside world fully clothed and prim. Women such as these are usually his regular customers.

Desire is a thing disguised in various forms. He delights greatly in the hunt. Usually this means he needs to probe in so many ways under equally many pretexts. It is the fact that he sees with his hands that he would go beyond the border—climbing up on the mounds, delving deep into the folds—and is excused for it. He is not worried about trespassing. His main concern is the period of time he's allowed within.

The moment he trespasses, every gesture and movement is critical. His touch needs to feign innocence (for how could he be excused otherwise?), but yet be calculated to catch it unguarded. He strives to stay, to linger, and to score. The 'game of hide-and-seek', he likes to call it.

A sharp intake of breath followed by a sigh, a groan—he wills and coaxes desire out of its cave. Behold the beautiful beast being exposed, reacting like a gnarling tigress, a strutting peacock, a bewildered dove, a hissing snake, a fiery lioness ...

To each, he bestows a distinctive name upon which his victory is marked. He selects these names with utmost care, for they represent that one moment of release and potential, never to be repeated. He is a proud keeper of these names—their ultimate sole guardian.

Little do the ladies of Jakarta's most elite class know that the blind masseur they frequent regularly in one of Kemang's exclusive spas (known and open to selected members only) is a father of three children and a respected member of his village near Malang—a man known for his quiet, elegant demure, eloquence and not insignificant contribution to the local projects (irrigation, mosques, schools) in the village and neighbouring regions.

Scene 4: Possession

Sometimes I really ask too much of you. I want to breathe you, I want to smile you, I want to linger you. It's the sweetness of love that I lick and suck till the juices run dry. (They never do run dry, and I don't ever get enough of you). You must be exhausted by me. I'm sorry for that.

I'm all yours completely and entirely—I like to say it though I don't know what that means. I like the sound of it. I like the idea of it. I like the idea of you. And me. Being us.

Some days, I feel you are not quite with me and that's when I scramble around fidgeting; what other things could you possibly have outside of me? Outside of us—don't really know what 'us' means, though I like to stress it. There's only us and more of us to come. It's an ancient thing, I know you would say, but so profound, isn't it—you and me becoming us?

I know I'm idiotic, but I really can't stand the idea of you not thinking of me, or not having me in your thoughts. How should that be allowed? I'm all yours completely and so are you mine. Just as we are one when we make love (how you embrace and grip me inside you!), why should it be any different when we are not in bed?

I don't like, I hate, how you lean towards a person as though at any time he can swoon you helplessly away. Don't you see my panic, my doom? I'm frantic; I know you will say that. I know half the things you will say—don't you see how well I know you? I am you, I am you, I am you. Now you roll your eyes and look away, and I sigh deeply for I have lost you again.

'Let's go to Puncak?' No.

'Bandung?' No.

'Bali, Lombok, Medan?' No, No, No.

'Let's get married?' (Two scenarios. One: you bulge your eyes at me and walk away, I run after you, pretend I haven't said anything. Two: you laugh and say 'Sure', I quickly get on my knees, kneel and kiss you all over.)

Only instead: 'Let's catch a movie at Plaza Indonesia?' and you let me grab your hand and lead you along.

Tomorrow, surely, you will be more mine than today.

Scene 5: The Sea

Once upon a time there lived a village in the Indo-Malay region who worshipped the Sea. The latter, with its tempestuous mood swings, is a vast forbidding presence to the villagers who cower themselves away upon seeing a sheer flash of lightning in its horizon. Trembling, they would cover their heads, shut their eyes tight, mutter prayers and chants. It is not obvious what it is of the Sea that they fear, for they settle quite a distance away from the coast and they certainly don't rely on it for their living. They are neither swimmers nor fishermen.

But for every little disaster that falls upon them, it is the image of the Sea's silvery claws crawling underneath and its thundering wrath that shake their conscience and make them kneel for forgiveness—though it is not apparent what misdeeds they have done to earn this reprimand.

Once the Sea stole upon them and took their animals, children, elders and weak ones. Convinced it was the end of their days, they waited for the Sea to sweep their remaining lot away.

Weeks and months passed without work, without sleep. But the Sea remained calm and unaffected. Coupled with clear blue skies twinkling shine on its undulating surface, it seemed content and pleased even.

Observing this agreeable mood, it was then agreed among the villagers that what they needed to do was offer gifts to the Sea. It was also agreed that it should be done at each complete cycle of the moon. With this resolution, the villagers recommenced their daily routine, taking comfort from the ritual sacrifices they communally made to the Sea.

On a slab of rock beaten by waves, kneeling over the sprawled lifeless body, he caressed and admired the soft features of her nose, mouth and cheeks. His palms pressed on her breasts, then her belly, futilely stroking and massaging them. As he entered her, he met his face with hers turned everlastingly silent towards the sea and whispered in his native tongue his desire and worship of her. He stayed with her till dusk fell, when he had to continue on with his journey southwards to his people.

She blinked to a ray of sunlight resting on her wet eyelids. Quietness surrounded her. For a long while, she lay, unknown to herself if she were living or dead. Gradually, she heard sounds coming from the Sea and felt the wind on her cheeks. She was soon awakened to her arms, limbs, hands and feet. The entire weight of her body came to her. Feeling cold, weak and thirsty, she finally gathered herself up and treaded her way slowly towards the island.

It was her mother who first saw and quickly covered her naked body with a large piece of cloth. The night she was to be given to the Sea, she had said goodbye to her only daughter. The woman she now saw was not her daughter. She knew this as she led her into the house and rested her in her daughter's bed. The next day she was presented to the villagers who gazed at her with wonder and awe. Not a few thought of her as the incarnated goddess of the Sea or, if that's too big a thought, at least as the one chosen and favored by the Sea—but to what purpose they were not sure. She was feared and admired all at once.

Months passed. The woman who was her mother continued to care for her until it became clear to the villagers that a child of the Sea was to be expected.

They built a tall house for her to live with her son, with an altar erected at the front terrace for the villagers to offer prayers and sacrifices. She chose its location, on a steep cliff jutting outwards to the Sea. Every day, mother and son would climb down the cliff to the shore. Her son was nurtured by the Sea and grew from the Sea. They shared and taught what they knew to the villagers, who remained timid but, all the same, curious. Eventually, many of them learned to swim and, with their fine carpentry skills, built rafts and boats to venture further into the Sea. In no time, the entire village was converted to swimmers and fishermen who no longer trembled before the Sea, but embraced her moods along with the riches she yielded.

Some nights lit by the full moon, the woman would be seen on the shore with her knees bent and spread wide apart. Waves, one after another, lapped in and out, over her legs, thighs and belly, as she hums her song of gratitude, homage and desire for her ethereal lover.

On these nights, many women lose virginity to their pining lovers and many widows seek comfort from friends and strangers alike. And the sounds coming from the Sea gently rock and cradle the villagers to sleep.

Suzanna Kusuma was born in Indonesia. She has a degree in English Literature and Philosophy from Australia and Holland. Currently based and working in Singapore, she writes poetry and other creative pieces during her leisure time. This is her first publication.

PHILIPPINES

Eduardo's Honeymoon

Annabel Pagunsan

Eduardo Cendrars Queral paid little attention to the usual landing announcements made by the flight crew as the Cebu Pacific Air jet began its descent over Mactan Island, its colourful yellow-and-orange livery flashing brightly in the tropical sunshine.

The Spaniard was more interested in watching Mi-chan's reactions to the sea of green that was becoming visible as the plane began to descend below the clouds. Her hand was resting on his thigh, hidden by the salmon-pink newsprint of the financial paper which he had lowered rather quickly over his lap when, at 25,000 feet, she had begun to worry and tease the head of his *batuta* with her elegant fingers.

His feet in their dark socks were still locked discreetly around one of her ankles; a delicate bare sole was pressed against his instep, exciting him even more than her pretty toes, which were curling softly as she caressed his foot lazily with them.

They were not the only couple on the flight in that kind of mood. After all, Cebu was a popular honeymoon destination, and the flight from Singapore was carrying the usual numbers of foreign newlyweds in every row.

However, Eduardo's honeymoon in Cebu was not going to be a typical tourist's *luna de miel*, either. For the first time in his life, he was bringing a wife to meet the Filipino side of the family. He was well into his forties, lean, and worldly; Mi-chan was only 23, and even more worldly than he was.

He was proud of her, and not only on account of her exotic Eurasian features and her pornographic curves; she had been educated well by the cousin who had raised her after she was orphaned. However, he had been thinking of the Filipino saying *may tainga ang lupa, may pakpak ang balita* even before they boarded the aircraft. 'The earth itself has ears, and gossip has wings.'

For his bride was gloriously and healthily pregnant, already in her second trimester, and the first time the family had ever heard of her was approximately three weeks previously, when he had telephoned his grandfather in Cebu to inform him that he was about to enter into a civil marriage with a young Frenchwoman who lived in Singapore.

Acting on a gut feeling, Eduardo had taken a deep breath and mentioned to his *lolo* that Mi-chan was very young, and was rather obviously *embarazada*; at least four months along, to be precise.

* * *

The grandfather they were going to visit in Cebu was a *tisoy*, the local term for a *mestizo* of European descent. Although the Filipino side of the family did not import their brides from Spain by design, a family tradition of sending the sons to the Old World for their education had meant that most of the men—including Eduardo's father and even the grandfather in Cebu—had chosen their wives from good Castilian, Basque or Catalan families in Spain.

Eduardo was a Spanish Filipino whose eyes were such a deep shade of blue that they looked almost violet; his looks were utterly Castilian. Although he still thought and dreamed in Spanish, and did most of his business in English or Japanese, his fluency in Cebuano and Ilonggo was well appreciated in the Philippines, where most of his workforce was based. His core business trained and employed dozens of talented local illustrators who worked on the animated feature films he produced with his Japanese partner.

* * *

Mi-chan had never visited the Philippines before, despite the fact that she had been living in Southeast Asia for nearly three years. After the prim efficiency of her adopted city of Singapore, she found herself enjoying the untidy bustle of Cebu-Mactan International Airport. Eduardo used his burgundy EU passport, instead of the maroon one issued by the Republika ng Pilipinas, so that he could be in the same queue as his wife.

Most of the passengers who had been on their flight were met by hotel staff in the airport terminal and herded into minibuses and hotel cars within a matter of minutes. Eduardo was queuing up patiently at the car rental booth when he was approached by a cheerful young Filipino who addressed him by name.

The man's name was Fidel. Smiling, Fidel greeted Mi-chan politely before saying, 'Sir Eduardo, your *lolo* wants me to drive you and Ma'am Ayumi to the house. He said to tell you that he doesn't trust your driving.'

Eduardo was bewildered, but understood perfectly when the driver continued, 'And he also asked me to tell you that your brother Juan Carlos and Ma'am Christine arrived the day before yesterday.'

The Spaniard shot a sympathetic look at Fidel, and asked him a pithy question in the Cebuano dialect, 'I suppose my brother's wife is in ... the usual form?'

'Oh yes, Sir,' was the young man's sunny reply.

* * *

The grandfather had asked to receive them privately in his study before they saw to any other family business—such as the complicated, and very public, distribution of *pasalubong*, the obligatory presents expected of any Filipino returning home. Mi-chan had brought him a fine hand-turned Danish pipe which she had purchased in Singapore.

Mi-chan watched her husband greet his *lolo* respectfully by making a slight bow over the back of the man's right hand, until the knuckles grazed his forehead. Acting on instinct, she copied the *mano po*, and received a very proper but affectionate *bisou* on each cheek from the grandfather in return.

At 92, Old Man Queral was a charmer. He also had an impish style about him which she had never detected in the grandson, who had a taste for aggressive martial arts, tended to take everything very seriously, and had certain rather dark hungers in the bedroom which some women might find intimidating.

Addressing his new granddaughter-in-law, the *lolo* said, 'My dear, let me give you my blessings for your marriage to my grandson. He is a lucky man. I understand that your parents are no longer living. I will do my best to make sure that their souls are at ease as long as you are here under my roof.'

He continued, 'I have explained to the family—especially the *titas*, who are anxious to meet you—that you are an expectant mother, and may want to rest until the *meryenda* at 4.30pm. The *pasalubong* and the introductions can wait, no?'

The lolo took Ayumi's hand and said, 'Thank you for the pipe, it is such a good one. Mrs Hizon has set out some refreshments in your room in case you get hungry or thirsty.'

* * *

The room which had been assigned to them was one of the most romantic rooms in the colonial-style *bahay na bato*—or 'house of stone'. That part of the house was so old that the afternoon light filtered into the room through panes made from translucent *capiz* shells, *ventanillas* carved from Philippine hardwoods, and colourful sheets of speckled glass.

Mi-chan lay back contentedly on the big four-poster bed and allowed her husband to remove her sandals and pull her panties down towards her ankles. He left on the confining Japanese *hara-obi* bindings which she insisted on winding tightly around her midriff after every bath in order to support the ever-growing bump and her lower back.

Eduardo's sexual hunger liquefied his wife's spine when he forced her young thighs apart with his knee and began to push the heavy head of his cock into her *kiki*, which was hot and fluid from the hormones.

The belly was high and narrow, in that modern way; soon he had her on her side, with her thighs parted widely and the bump pressed safely to the side, and was thrusting into her in a rough rhythm which made her full breasts roll heavily into his hands as he smacked his hips against her buttocks and her thighs.

One of his hands gripped her ankle and pulled it back in order to open her up more as he ploughed her young body with his *batuta*, a Spanish Filipino word meaning 'baton'.

In the gentle tropical heat of the afternoon—which was kept comfortably at bay by one ageing air-conditioning unit that juddered every few minutes as it kept the bedroom well-chilled, in true Filipino style—Mi-chan moaned softly as her husband made love to her. At one point, the *butiki*—house geckos—scurrying silently along the walls and across the ceilings watched Eduardo strip the pregnancy girdle from his wife's midriff and use that to tie her to the bedposts.

After the sex, Mi-chan sat quietly on a low stool in the simple old-fashioned bathroom as Eduardo lathered their bodies up with a bar of soap and rinsed the suds off, Filipino-style, with big scoops of fresh water from a large earthenware jar fed by a plastic hose attached directly to the faucet.

The slippery feel of her warm soapy body under his hands brought the Spaniard's *dako* back to life yet again, and Mi-chan was quite happy to find herself being eased, monkey-style, onto a very clean penis which spread her buttocks as her husband asserted his conjugal rights on the cool bathroom tiles.

*   *   *

The *meryenda* was Ayumi's formal introduction to the family. In Spain, a *merienda* was a simple affair, a piece of fruit and some toast or pastries served with coffee or tea just before sundown.

In Old Man Queral's household, this snack was a substantial meal, Filipino style, with custard tarts, Chinese meat buns, a healthy selection of fresh tropical fruit, and even a steaming dish of fried *pancit* noodles. Although sundown was still a couple of hours away, both he and Eduardo accepted the tumblers of whiskey offered to them by the staff; Mi-chan sipped a glass of young coconut juice.

Eduardo's brother Juan Carlos looked longingly at the drinks tray, but settled on a glass of fresh pineapple juice after a sharp remark from his wife. The servants were all aware that Juan Carlos was living *under the saya*, although they would never dream of expressing those views in so many words. To say, even jokingly, that a man lived under his woman's skirts—her *saya*—was quite a serious insult in the Philippines.

Christine was the kind of Frenchwoman for whom the air-conditioning in Cebu was never cold enough and for whom the staff never moved quickly enough. She and Juan Carlos lived in France; the only thing she enjoyed about visiting the *hacienda* in Cebu was having a large staff to boss about.

Old Man Queral often wondered why Christine was so imperious and demanding with his staff when, in France, she washed her own clothes and relied on a cleaner who came in two days a week. Her behaviour always reminded him of the Phillipine saying 'A fly that lands on a carabao feels itself to be higher than the carabao.'

* * *

The woman began attacking Mi-chan almost as soon as the family was seated around the mango wood table on the patio. During their first meeting only the week before, Juan Carlos had been taught by Eduardo to treat Mi-chan with respect, but his wife was not a fast learner.

Christine's line of attack was the pregnancy. Under the pretext of being happy for Ayumi, she seized every opportunity to draw attention to the healthy size of the bride's stomach, considering that she had been married for only a few weeks. Her remarks injured Eduardo's pride, his *amor proprio*; the Filipino sense of embarrassment and shame, called *hiya*, was deeply ingrained in him.

Mi-chan, who understood the Asian concept of 'face' perfectly, sensed that her husband was not in a position to put Christine in her place without losing even more face. For his sake, she concentrated on maintaining a sweet, calm and respectful demeanour.

Old Man Queral liked the way Mi-chan was holding on to her dignity. Unlike Christine, who was rapidly approaching what Filipino culture calls the *napasubo*, the ominous 'point of no return' in social conflict; the aunts, uncles and cousins at the table were already looking embarrassed and uncomfortable.

He had thought well of Eduardo's young bride from the moment she had greeted him instinctively with a *mano po*, a simple but meaningful gesture which Juan Carlos' wife had never bothered to perform.

Just as he was about to say something firm to Christine to

put a stop to the nonsense once and for all, Mi-chan spoke up. 'Grandfather, I feel very embarrassed to present myself at your house in this condition.' She added, wistfully, 'My stomach is so big. *O-negai shimasu*; I am sorry.'

Her words snapped every head in her direction. Including the household staff. The head of the family raised his glass to his new granddaughter-in-law and smiled at her. '*Hija*,' he said, 'all that matters to me is that both you and the baby are well. I have never seen my grandson so happy before. And he is no fool.'

In an instant, the old man's gracious words made Christine's pointed remarks appear indelicate, and even uncouth. The formal afternoon tea continued without further incident.

* * *

Mi-chan enjoyed her stay at the Spanish-style colonial house where she spent her time getting to know the grandfather who had shaped her husband's character, and gaining a feel for the rhythms of life in Central Visayas, which was colourful and lush beyond anything she had imagined when she had chosen to make tropical Singapore her home.

The honeymoon in Cebu showed her a side of her husband which she had not known when they were in Europe. He seemed more playful—and, well, *Asian*—in the Philippines, especially when he spoke in Filipino.

She could not bring herself to tease him when, on the very first day of their stay, he had approached her, looking sheepish, and handed her a small cloth pouch containing a knob of ginger and a few coins, which one of the older servants had asked him to keep close to her pillow as protection against the *asuwang*, a deadly supernatural creature which is believed to feed on pregnant women and their unborn children after dark.

His lovemaking was sweeter and rougher and deeper in the New World; the long and quiet siesta period every afternoon was always well-used by them. The Japanese pregnancy girdle was unwound every day between two and four in the afternoon. He enjoyed the pregnant sex so much that he even entertained inappropriate thoughts of keeping Mi-chan *embarazada* all the time.

During their honeymoon on the *hacienda*, Eduardo and his new bride went at it like Sikalak and Sikabay, the Adam and Eve of the Visayas creation myth, who made so many babies that the pale-skinned Spanish conquistadors who arrived in the 16th century were initially believed to be the descendants of Aryon, the son who had travelled north to lands so cold that the winds there had blown all good sense out of his head.

* * *

One hot afternoon, a few days into the honeymoon, Mi-chan sent her husband off to play golf with his friends, under the pretext that she needed to rest. Eduardo returned to the house sun-burned and sweaty and happy after 18 holes of golf at the course in Danao City.

He found a note from her on the bed. 'Out shopping with Tita Ernesta. Back at 4.00. See you—Mi-chan.' Grinning, he headed for the shower, leaving the bathroom door ajar so that he could hear his wife letting herself in, exactly 30 minutes later. For she was always punctual, even in the Philippines, where timekeeping was elastic.

Eduardo hummed under the cool water as he soaped himself, feeling very pleased with himself for having been intelligent enough to marry a young woman who had a wise old head on her slim shoulders, and tastes which were such a good match for his hungers. Drying himself off with a towel, he stepped into the bedroom and was so startled to see his wife standing there that he bit his lip.

Mi-chan had her hair in a ponytail, and she was wearing a cheerleader outfit, a very distinctive one in a rich shade of Marian Blue, which he knew well from his days at the Ateneo de Manila— right down to the white shoes and socks. He wondered how she even knew about the famous cheerleaders of his alma mater's *Ateneo Blue Eagles*.

When he approached her, she signalled to him to stop. He obeyed. Hoisting one small, white-clad foot onto a chair, she pretended to adjust a shoelace, exposing a great deal of fair silky thigh and a sliver of navy blue panties.

Smiling naughtily, Mi-chan shocked his stiff penis to full attention by executing a near-perfect *herkie* for him to see. On landing, she took two graceful steps forward, lifted one long leg, and rested a neatly be-socked ankle on his shoulder, allowing the skimpy pleats of her skirt to plunge to her crotch. She was very agile despite the expanding stomach, which was already quite solid and growing by the day.

Kissing his new wife very deeply on the mouth, Eduardo used his hands to rub her between her supple legs over the dark blue cotton of her panties, lingering at the very damp spot just below her clit.

Mi-chan decided that it was time to progress matters. Removing her ankle from his shoulders, she kept the hungry Spaniard back with one slim arm held straight out, and leaned back until her lovely ass was resting against the edge of the small table where Mrs Hizon had laid out a tray of fruit and tea things.

Eduardo stepped forward very quickly and dropped to his knees in front of her. He was still naked and damp from the shower; he had lost his towel and his solid *pokochin* was pointing straight ahead.

Pulling the panties down those tender thighs, and leaving them beached at her knees, he began to work on his wife with his mouth. Using both thumbs to stretch her sweet baby lips lengthwise, he flicked his tongue firmly along, and even into, the lips which were being pulled gently taut, making her shudder and mew as he ate and drank her hungrily.

Once again, Mi-chan changed gears for both of them. Kicking off her white sneakers, she gripped the sides of his head hard and pushed him and his prickly blue chin back far enough to place one small foot against his chest and push him back onto his heels.

The white sock travelled steadily from his very Spanish chest down to his groin, where she used her foot to play with his *chinchin-san* until *Little Eduardo* was furiously hard. The husband gripped her lower thigh with his hand, making her shiver as he stroked and squeezed the soft back of her knee.

Eduardo broke free of Mi-chan's leg, rising to his feet above her so quickly that he was able to make her gasp sharply by spinning her around and flipping up her tiny skirt. He gripped her firmly with one arm around her waist, trapping her, as he bent her—and that belly of hers—forward over the desk.

He only needed the long fingers of one hand to spread her buttocks; Mi-chan was always crazy for anal sex. And her sexual hunger was so great these days, in the second trimester, as the hormones heated her skin and turned it to velvet, thickened her hair, and engorged her nipples and the tender membranes between her legs.

As usual, Eduardo paused for a moment to enjoy an intimate look at the woman he was about to take.

And was startled to see something sparkle between his wife's buttocks. He was puzzled for only a few moments.

Pushing his nose and mouth deep between her cheeks, Eduardo prickled and grazed her briefly with his stubble as he worked his teeth around the edges of the small round diamond and platinum stud covering her sphincter.

He tugged gently with his mouth, drawing out a small platinum plug so slowly with his teeth that Ayumi's knees trembled; his hand had moved to the front of her crotch and was very busy there.

Rising to his feet, Eduardo held his wife's chin gently as she received the plug from his mouth, the contact between their lips making him so aroused that he left the jewellery between her teeth, braced his hand across her throat, and felt the vibrations of her moans through his fingers as he pushed his penis deep inside her back entrance.

No lubrication; he barely allowed her the time to adjust to his cock's rude entry before he began to take her with long fast strokes, vaguely aware that the hem of her skirt was brushing against the base of his penis, increasing his pleasure. Eduardo knew that the sounds coming from her were a mixture of a bit of pain and a great deal of pleasure.

The arm around her waist shifted to her chest as the rhythm of his thrusts became quite fierce; Mi-chan was having to rise on tiptoe now with every stroke. The fingers he was keeping between her legs were signalling to him that she was shivering on the verge of a very nice orgasm.

Biting his wife's shoulder hard enough to make her yelp once as she squirmed against that big cock in her butt and began to come, Eduardo swung his hips firmly upwards twice, thrusting roughly between her cheeks as he spurted inside her with such force that he began to feel a slow trickle of himself ooze out between her tightly-stretched muscles and his shaft.

Panting, Eduardo stopped thrusting so that he could enjoy the sensation of his cock throbbing inside her as it softened; both husband and wife could feel the baby kicking. He kissed Mi-chan and thanked her for the nice welcome home.

They had at least one free hour to themselves before they had to dress for the next *meryenda* at the mango wood table on the patio. His heart pounding as if he had just completed a fierce and aggressive session of *kendo* with his Japanese business partner, Eduardo fondled his wife's breasts and listened to the white cockatoos quarrelling and making love outside the finely carved *ventanillas* of the room which was home to both him and Mi-chan during his honeymoon in Cebu. He felt very contented.

Annabel Pagunsan is the pseudonym of a Singapore-based author of literary erotica. AP is currently working on the second and third novels in the 'Patrick & Ayumi: Hard-working Slaves' series.

Max In Waiting

Nigel Hogge

Max sped to the sofa, just in time to be there when the delicious young woman arrived with his second martini, and just in time to catch the visual feast offered him again. As he accepted his drink, which he noticed was a double, two thoughts crossed his slightly befuddled mind. Firstly, this wasn't his second martini, it was his fifth of the night … and secondly, Leah's breasts had grown larger, if that was possible since his first … no, his fourth martini.

'Thank you, my dear girl,' he said pompously, then stuck his finger into the cold silvery liquid and clumsily swirled it around, disturbing the olive.

The girl straightened and stepped back from the sofa. 'I shall go to my room now, Mister Max. Roberto will wait at the gate. Please stay here if you wish. Perhaps you can sleep for a moment.'

'Yes, I'll wait. I can do nothing else.'

The girl left. Max rose and called his own apartment. Gloria had a key to his front door, the only woman who did. No answer.

He called the hotel bar again. She hadn't arrived, and according to the bartender's tone of voice, wouldn't. He watched TV and finished the drink. He was sloshed. Zapped. Fried. He closed his eyes.

One of the lights in the living room went out. He opened his eyes with a start. He had been dozing. Leah was standing next to the TV. In the light thrown from the screen, he saw she was wearing a long nightgown made of cotton. The material was thin and he saw, very clearly, the shape of her legs and buttocks through the fabric. She turned off the set and the room fell dark, lit only by a soft lamp in the far corner of the spacious living room.

'Leah, I thought you had gone to bed.'

His voice sounded harsh. His mouth felt dry. He was unable to pull his eyes away from the girl's nightie. She looked very pretty. Her hair fell in inky waves down her back. Neglecting to answer him, she walked to the window and looked out, perhaps searching for the figure of Roberto up the driveway. She drew the curtains closed.

They were maroon silk, matching the sofa on which he slumped. To close them, she stood on tip-toes, reaching up and struggling with the heavy material, and Max could see, through the soft near darkness, the bunched muscles of her rounded bottom under the cheap cotton, and below that, her strong calf muscles and the adorable white soles of her bare feet.

He groaned and sat up straight, his hand knocking over the empty martini glass. He felt woozy and very, very horny. He looked down at the bulge under the gray material of his slacks. His dick was a stiff pole.

'My God,' he said to himself. 'I'm waiting for my date in her house. She has disappeared into thin air. She could show up at any moment. Behave yourself.'

But then another extremely cunning thought crossed his mind. If Gloria does return ... no, *when* Gloria returns in her BMW ... I shall hear the engine revving, a door slamming, footsteps on the gravel, a front door opening. The curtains are closed and ...

'Come here, Leah.'

But the girl was already kneeling in front of him, between his knees. Her dark eyes, so innocent before, now searched his with all the knowledge of woman, woman eternal. He stroked her hair.

'Leah ...'

The girl placed a finger on his lips. 'Don't talk, Mister Max. I must tell you a secret.'

'What secret, little one? If you tell me, it won't be a secret, will it?'

Shut up, Max, he told himself.

'The secret is I love you. I have loved you since I first saw you here with Ma'am Gloria.'

'That's silly. I'm much older than you.'

Jesus, man, keep quiet.

'It doesn't matter, Mister Max. Anyway, where I come from in Benedet, girls get married much younger than I am now. Don't you like me? Am I not pretty enough for you?'

'Oh, you're *beautiful*. So beautiful.' It was true.

Leah smiled. 'So? It could be our secret. Roberto is at the gate, Missy and Livian are sleeping long ago. May I kiss you?'

'You may.'

He pulled her off her knees. She hiked up her nightdress, so that it bunched around her hips. He gasped. She straddled him, one knee on either side of him on the sofa, and placed her soft lips on his. They kissed deeply. His hands went around her. His strong arms hugged her tightly. She felt incredibly warm and soft and wonderful.

She moved back, looked down and unzipped his slacks. Finding what she searched for, she gently pulled his rigid barnstormer out and stroked it. She moved up and forward, panting and shifting her buttocks urgently.

His hands slid up her brown legs. They felt silkier than the couch he was sitting on. He grasped her plump bottom cheeks under the nightie. She sank, moaning, onto his cock.

It entered her hot, wet cave of dreams. Her pussy was so smooth and liquid that he speared her without effort. She cried out.

He grunted. In his half-drunken state, he thought he had never felt anything so fabulous in his stormy life. He rammed himself all the way in, then she rose up, holding his shoulders for support and began sinking down and rising up at an ever increasing pace, and in this manner the two of them fucked madly while waiting for Gloria Jacobi Dupree to return.

Their senses were incredibly alive, the danger of discovery at the back of their giddy, pleasure-crazed minds as she writhed and moaned and lifted her nightdress over her shoulders and head and cast it onto the sofa and she was naked while he guzzled at her huge breasts as they leapt in front of him.

His eyes closed as he kissed and licked them and she cried, 'Yes, yes, Mister Max, oh yes, kiss them, kiss them,' as her bottom cheeks jolted and tightened and loosened and her fingers tore his shirt open and she bent to kiss his hairy chest, then raised her face to suck his lips and bite them and thrust her wet tongue into his throat and the heat rose and it was too late to hold on as they both came with frantic, strangled shouts of glee, they yelped and groaned their way to fruition and slumped and sagged on the couch.

Leah fell off him and sprawled on the carpet. Time passed. Max's sodden night warrior slowly subsided until it lolled damply against his slacks. The skipper slipped it back where it had come from and zipped himself up. He could get back to waiting for his lovely date to arrive home.

Nigel Hogge, born on the Isle of Wight in 1942, has worked as a fisherman and miner in Australia, a manager of a copra plantation in New Guinea, a tourist guide in Hong Kong, an English teacher in Tokyo, a bartender in Los Angeles, a seaman on a Swedish cargo vessel and a sales representative in Korea and Vietnam. He has been the 'voice' on over 250 radio and TV commercials in Manila and Tokyo, a character actor in more than 15 movies, he has written and sold four movie scripts, and he now lives on his 57-foot cabin cruiser in the southern Philippines. *Max in Waiting* is excerpted from the novel *Lucifer Rising* (Charleston: BookSurge, 2003).

Night Ride

Nigel Hogge

The gears of the old diesel engine clashed and the bus lumbered off up the highway, bumping over potholes and creaking from side to side. Lisa fought her way to the rear to see if she could get a last fond look at her mother and sisters, but when she got there, the gathering dusk made it impossible to see anything through the grimy rear window.

For some reason she began to cry. Perhaps it was a memory of her father averting his eyes as he accepted the little gift from her that started the tears. She searched for tissue paper in her purse, all that she carried besides an overnight bag and some ears of corn bound with twine, pressed upon her by her mother at the bus stop.

A hand loomed in front of her face, holding a handkerchief. Instinctively, she took it and wiped her eyes. Pulling herself together, she removed the cloth from her face and was disturbed to see it wasn't very clean.

She turned to the person who had so kindly offered it to her and was surprised to see a young foreigner, a tall, skinny white guy dressed in a faded denim jacket, scruffy white T-shirt and khaki shorts. He was grinning at her. In the darkness, she could make out faint pockmarks on his face. He had a big, thick-lipped mouth that reminded her of an English rock-and-roll star she'd seen cavorting on a video.

She quickly returned the grubby cloth, nodded curtly, and turned back to the window. She was in no mood for banter. She felt depressed and stared through the glass at the occasional passing light.

The bus droned on through the evening. Night fell. Her feet ached. She hung onto the ceiling strap for support, and out of nowhere her depression lifted, and wicked, erotic thoughts came to her, the kind of thoughts that often plagued her because she was, she knew, a wicked and erotic girl.

Wild fantasies entered her mind, not helped by the fact that she was standing on a filthy floor which trembled and vibrated and sent tremors running up her legs, finishing up at the same damp spot between her luscious, plump, quivering thighs.

Naughty visions of men, boys, hairy chests, flat bellies, hard biceps, lean buttocks, swelling calf muscles, corded necks, thick wrists, sensitive fingers, firm jaws, the feel of a man's ... *caramba*!!

She froze, her cheek pressed to the unclean glass ... *caramba*! The son of a bitch! The low-down animal! Was she imagining this, or was this part of a dream? Had she fallen asleep standing, and what she felt pressed against her bottom just imagination?

She unwrapped the green leaves from a sheath of ripe yellow corn and wondered if she shouldn't offer some to the foreigner standing behind her. He had been silent so far, thank the Lord, and she couldn't be sure whether he was very kind or a disgusting pervert. She decided to keep the rest of the corn to give to her girlfriends at the club, and sank her pearly white teeth into the soft, delicious flesh of ... *caramba*!

Placed against her butt, which she knew from experience was one of her most sought-after features, was a warm iron pipe. Yes, right in the groove between her bottom cheeks! She chewed on the corn furiously.

She couldn't scream for help with her mouth full. She twisted her head around to glare at the white guy, but he was standing with his eyes closed, a peaceful, innocent expression painted on his face, which was definitely not handsome. The warm iron pipe had withdrawn. It no longer pushed against her soft rump. She stared up at the man for a while. It was too dark to see if he was pretending to be dozing. A car passed the bus and the cabin was momentarily lit, the yellow glare of the passing headlights sweeping across the mass of long-suffering humanity squeezed like cattle inside the bus as it rattled through the hot night towards the capital.

She blinked and was startled to see his eyes, which were a deep brown with flecks of gold, now open and looking at her.

They didn't turn away. The man watched her, no longer grinning like an idiot. He wasn't quite as unattractive as she had first thought. She frowned at him and turned back to her solitary vigil at the greasy window. She knew what would happen next ... and it did.

Actually, two things happened at the same time. She had just realized that her pussy was very wet because of the nasty thoughts she'd been unable to banish from her mind minutes earlier, when the bus hit a particularly large pothole on the highway and the foreigner was thrown against her back. A growl of irritation rose from the passengers, and some of the peasants near the front of the bus told the driver their opinions of his ancestry and his mother's true occupation, but what Lisa knew with total clarity was that the iron pipe against her rump was real, very real, and had not been a dream.

The man groaned, inches from the back of her head, and what did little Miss Catholic Country Girl do? What did prim and proper Miss Irritation do? She pressed her bottom back against his penis, is what she did.

To this day, when she thought about that moment, which was often, she could hardly suppress a smile. It was a delicious moment. The fire in her belly churned, the torment between her legs itched so much that she had to twist herself against the side of the bus.

She dropped the corn husk and her purse and raised her hand to the strap above her, the better to display herself for the foreigner's pleasure. Standing on tip-toes, her calf muscles taut, she firmly, without a hint of shame, hidden by the noisy darkness, moved her *derriere* against his dick and began rubbing herself up and down like a mare in heat cajoling a stallion, for in heat she was.

She was wearing a red blouse made of silky material and although it was demure in style, with long sleeves and a big collar, she could actually look down and see her nipples pushing through the fabric. She placed a hand on her left breast and teased the stiff, thrusting peak of her nipple, playing with it, pinching, tweaking the small living cone, then, moving her fingers to the other breast, repeated the torment.

Her breath was rapid, further fogging the glass inches in front of her mouth. The hefty meat of the stranger's prick gave off such a heat as to warm her bottom. The two of them, existing in their sensual zone of privacy amongst this mass of flesh around them ... a zone made all the more thrilling because of its proximity to danger and discovery ... began to move in time with the bus's lurching motion.

His hands, unable to restrain themselves, left the strap and used her shoulders, and then her waist, for support. He leaned into her, and her bottom clenched and unclenched as his turgid love club, so fearfully constrained by the cloth of his khaki pants, pushed against her black skirt and silk panties, layers of material it was desperate to break through. Suddenly, the bus swerved off the highway and bumped down a short track to pull up, with a groan of brakes and a sigh from the ancient transmission, at a dimly lit way-station.

The bus stopped and the passengers pushed and jostled towards the door, which had swung open with a bang. Within seconds, they were alone on the vehicle, save for the baskets of vegetables and fruits, the slatted crates of chickens and a few pigs tethered by their hind legs.

She leaned down to pick up her purse, fighting to control her pumping breath, conscious of the soggy sweetness between her inner thighs, hardly able to turn from the window and escape her torturer. But turn she did, and fled, unable to make eye contact with the man, so shy did she now feel.

She climbed down the steps shakily and walked towards a soft drink stand. She didn't know how long she stood staring at the rows of bottles, back-lit by the flickering oil lamps of the tiny cafe. People milled about as night moths flew around her head and around the soft, hissing glow of the lamps. She was lost in a personal trance, the feel of the man's mighty cock alive in her memory. She forced herself to drink a bottle of sugary soda. She paid for it with trembling hands and entered the forest behind the cafe to take a pee before returning to the bus.

As she strolled back to the dusty vehicle, she saw the man leaning against a tree. In front of him he held a big suitcase. She guessed he might have travelled a long way. What route had he taken that fate had planted him so near to her on this night? Where was he coming from? Where was he going? She smiled at him timidly, but his eyes were averted. She knew the suitcase was held in front of him to conceal the bulge in his shorts.

The driver of the bus shouted and clapped his hands. They were on their way again, ready for the final hour's drive through Manaha's morbid outskirts and from there to the center of the city, and she had a decision to make.

Would she, could she, return to the back of the bus to take up her former position by the window? Would he follow her? Should she stand, this time, at the front of the vehicle to escape him? Was she a slut or was she a decent Verubian *whore on the way back to peddle herself once more along the dangerous waterfront of the capital*? Was she losing her mind?

She sprang onto the bus near the head of the line of passengers and strode back to her original place. A small smile was upon her lips. So she was a slut after all. So be it. She could hardly wait for the man. She knew with the female's carnal intuition that he would soon be behind her again. She knew his need, and needed that need.

She knew he was there as the bus thumped and jolted back to the highway, stopped, changed gears with a hydraulic hiss, and swung to the left to begin its final lap of the night. Her dark, pretty eyes lit up with an inner fire as once again his manhood pressed against her jouncing young bottom cheeks.

But this time the playing was over. She had signalled her permission. She had, in effect, surrendered any rights she might have as a young girl travelling alone in the night, a citizen of this country, a human being going about legal business. No, that was gone.

His strong hands pulled the black hem of her skirt up and took the elastic band of her panties and slipped them down. She gasped and wriggled. One of her hands dropped from the strap to curl behind her and place itself on the marvellous length of his dagger, and the feel of it was breathtaking.

The man was wasting no more time, an urgency was upon him, a grim need, as his hand took her wrist and assisted her in unbuttoning the buttons of his military type shorts with their safari pockets.

The buttons were swiftly opened and his weapon, smooth and helmeted, truly a warrior in the night, thick and veined, fell from his pants, jerking and twitching into her hand. She whimpered and turned and was lifted onto his suitcase, which was kicked under her by his booted foot, and she was now face to face with the enemy and her arms went around his sweet bony body.

She felt his ribs through the T-shirt and put her hands under the shirt to feel his muscular lean back, her hands hidden under the denim jacket ... Oh, Jesus, he felt so good, his skin was like a baby's, but so hot.

He was burning as she opened her legs like a shameless hussy, eager to be entered. His lips brushed her forehead and his fingers swept the black hair from her sparkling eyes.

She gazed with love, yes love, into his face, searching every wonderful imperfection of his features, her mouth hungry for the taste of his lips and tongue and ... dear God ... the helmet of his naked baton touched the soft hair of her snatch ... the man was going to fuck her! Not *here* ... please not now ... we'll be caught, she thought, her mind a turmoil. We'll be *seen*.

The bus will stop, people will shout and point, the police will arrive and lock them up like animals in a cage, her picture will be in the papers, her mother, her sisters ... no, worse, her poor *father* ... will see her stupid face plastered over every journal in the land. She'd be a laughing stock, totally notorious like one of those starlets she liked to read about and criticize ...

This was the end, she had to escape, she just *had* to, and ... it felt good, so good, as the length of his cock slipped one inch into her open, pulsating love lips. She stood on his suitcase, eyes glazed, lips wet, and eased slowly onto his cock.

She felt the ramrod enter her straight and in command. She was but its subject, its slave, two inches, three inches, and more, please free me from this pleasure, and suddenly he was all the way in, who knew how many inches now, and she felt the bigness and tightness, and felt she might die. It was too big, was she to be slaughtered by this animal, this white bastard was going to kill her, and then she began to pump with him, for him, around him, tightening her wicked quim, stroking his back, biting his mouth till she tasted salty blood, kissing him so she couldn't scream, her heart pounding as her orgasm came to her without warning.

Her round bottom, naked and squeezed and probed by the man's rough hands, was whipping back and forth as her orgasm grew and spread like molten lava through the pit of her belly. She felt her juice flow down the slippery sides of her secret place, she moaned in ecstasy and passed out for many seconds.

She didn't know and would never know how long she fainted because the bliss was so surreal, the delicious pain of it so maddening that she lost consciousness, and the man held her up, supported her with his wiry arms, one hand on her bare bottom, the other around her waist as spasm after spasm now hit *him*.

His froth flowed into her in creamy streaks, and because of their upright position and the laws of gravity, began to drip from her honey pot, overflowing from her forest of want, and streaks of it fell between their legs to land in drops onto the suitcase.

In their frenzied orbit of lust, she had stiffened at the feel of his hot come, her eyes rolling back to show the whites, and they hadn't realized that the bus had stopped at a red light and was stuck in a traffic jam.

The interior of the bus was now bathed in patches of moving light, for they had entered the city. Their frantic coupling must end and the cruelty of having their pleasure so abruptly taken from them was acute, but his dong, sodden and still huge, slipped out of her while the walls of her pussy tried to hold and clutch the big guy on its way out, pathetically attempting to prevent its escape.

But all men's cocks eventually must leave that sweet wound between the female's legs ... oh, would that they could remain in the moist, sumptuous havens of pussies forever, never having to face the harsh world again.

But such a mean trick had been played, so the young buck withdrew from Lisa, pulled his whanger out and wiped it with the same dank cloth he had earlier offered to dry her weeping eyes. He released her. She stepped off the suitcase, pulled up her panties, pushed down her skirt, and tugged her red blouse together where the buttons had been torn off. Rivulets of perspiration coursed down her face. They stood there, dazed. The rest of the journey passed quickly.

The bus stopped at the main terminal on Avenue De La Paz. They waited until the other passengers had alighted. Several of the country folk who had travelled with them gave the couple curious looks. Was it possible their ardor had been less furtive than they had presumed? It hardly mattered now. No one had raised an alarm. They calmly stepped from the bus and wandered onto the wide avenue, which was quiet at this time of night, save for the occasional passing vehicle. A light rain fell, creating haloes of light around the well-spaced street lamps. They stood on the sidewalk holding hands.

Nigel Hogge, born on the Isle of Wight in 1942, has worked as a fisherman and miner in Australia, a manager of a copra plantation in New Guinea, a tourist guide in Hong Kong, an English teacher in Tokyo, a bartender in Los Angeles, a seaman on a Swedish cargo vessel and a sales representative in Korea and Vietnam. He has been the 'voice' on over 250 radio and TV commercials in Manila and Tokyo, a character actor in more than 15 movies, he has written and sold four movie scripts, and he now lives on his 57-foot cabin cruiser in the southern Philippines. *Max in Waiting* is excerpted from the novel *In the Shadow of the Devil* (Charleston: BookSurge, 2003).

THAILAND

Banging Bill's Wife

Stephen Leather

This is the truth, the absolute truth, cross my heart and hope to die, as true as I'm sitting here. I can barely believe it myself, but it happened and it happened to me. The name's Adrian, better not tell you my surname because it's a small world. A bloody small world as it happens. I'm a stockbroker; usually I deal in shares, but I dabbled in bonds for a few years. Just on my way to my new job, and the company's paying, which is why I'm up here in Business Class and not in the back of the plane with the plebs.

I've done all right over the last few years, though I have had my share of setbacks, truth be told. I worked for Barings before they went bust, even worked in the same office as Nick Leeson for a while. Nice lad, was Nick, just got a bit out of his depth, that's all.

I worked for Lehman Brothers for two years, not long before they went out of business, and I was with a subsidiary of RBS in Hong Kong when they had to be bailed out by the British taxpayer. That's why my mates they call me Jonah. They reckon I'm cursed. They're joking, because I always make money for my bosses. Lots of money. I'm a rainmaker, that's why. I bring in the business. When I move, most of my clients move with me. That's what's going to happen this time, as sure as night follows day. Most of them, anyway.

I never really liked Singapore, the whole place changed after Barings went under, but I'll work anywhere providing the money's good. I was in Hong Kong, working in the bond department of Standard Chartered Bank, when I got headhunted by the Singapore firm. You always know when it's a headhunter on the phone. 'Can you talk?' they ask. Tossers. Of course I can talk. That what I do. I talk and people buy. It's called selling.

Anyway, I go in to see the headhunter and it turns out the guy doing the hiring used to be my boss at Barings, Chinese high-flyer by the name of Robert Tam. I always got on well with Robert, so I fly over to Singapore and he introduces me to the top guys and, of course, they offer me the job. More money, expat package, they'd even have paid for school fees if I'd had kids. The one problem was that my bosses in Hong Kong knew that I'd try to take my clients with them, so they had me out of the office as soon as I handed in my notice, and insisted that I couldn't start work in Singapore until my notice period was over. Three months.

They'd pay me and my bosses in Singapore said they'd pay me, too, so I was getting double salary but effectively I was on gardening leave. But I've always lived in flats and never had a garden, so I decided to spend three months in Thailand. I've done a few R&R runs to the Land of Smiles over the years, but I'd never spent any real time there, so I figured I'd go and blow off some steam. Singapore pays well, but it's not the most exciting city in the world for a single guy. I think maybe that was why Nick Leeson went off the rails.

Anyway, I booked myself into the Landmark Hotel on

Sukhumvit Road, between the red-light areas of Nana Plaza and Soi Cowboy, and started to let rip. Like a bull in a china shop. I did my rounds of the Bangkok bars, night after night in Nana Plaza, Soi Cowboy and Pat Pong. I went through the massage parlours, the short-time hotels, the go-go bars, hung around the freelance joints like Gullivers, the German Bar in Soi 7, the Bed Club and the nightclubs attached to the five-star hotels. I spent weekends in Pattaya, the sex-tourist's Disneyland-by-the-sea, non-stop sex fuelled by drink and drugs. In the first month alone, I went with more than a hundred girls. At least. To be honest, I lost count. I'd have breakfast, then a soapy massage, then a nap, then pick up a bargirl and take her to a short-time hotel, then have dinner and then go to a nightclub and pick up a freelancer. And that would be a quiet day. Sometimes in Pattaya I'd get laid four or five times, often with several girls at the same time.

I slowed down a little during the second month. I guess I was getting bored. Funny, right? Who would ever imagine that you'd get bored with sex? But that's what happened. There are only so many positions, only so many variations on a theme, and after a while it all became the same, pretty much. Drink, shower, sex, shower, sleep. And money always changed hands. I think that's what started to take the edge off it, the fact that I always paid. The girls smiled and laughed at my jokes and seemed to have a great time, but I was paying them. I began to realize that it was all about the money. No money, no honey.

That's when I discovered Craigslist. It's brilliant, Craigslist. Craigslist.org: none of that dot com nonsense for those guys. It's a website where you can buy or sell stuff, and where you can meet

107

people too. Real people. And if you're looking for free sex, then Craigslist is the place to go. I found it by accident. I think I was googling 'Free Porn' like I often do and it took me to a Craigslist page where a girl called Porn was looking for a date. She was a nurse at a Bangkok hospital and she was looking for a Caucasian guy with a good heart and I figured that two out of three was enough, so I called the mobile number, met her for coffee and an hour later, I was in her bed and between her legs. Sweet girl, and not very experienced despite her name. And she didn't ask me for money. Not one baht.

It was a one-night stand and the start of many, all courtesy of Craigslist. It was brilliant: hundreds of Thai birds gagging for it and not a penny to be paid. Most of the girls who posted put up their pictures so you could see what you were getting, and a few minutes on the phone was all it took to check that they were genuine. Then I'd go around to their place. I made that a rule. They never came to my hotel, I always went to them. That was one of the things that made it fun—you got to spend time in their world. Mind you, most of them lived in tiny studio flats full of stupid stuffed toys with posters of Korean boy bands on their walls, but that's not the point. I was getting to see real girls in their own homes and I was getting to bang them for free.

I slept with students, teachers, three air hostesses, half a dozen nurses, and even a policewoman; and yes, she wore the uniform and handcuffed me to the bed. I never told any of them my real name and I kept changing SIM cards because I didn't want then phoning me after the event. Besides, there was no need to make any return visits because there was a constant supply of fresh girls coming on line. Word was spreading that the website was a great way for Thai girls to meet Western guys and new girls were logging on every day.

After a few weeks, though, even the thrill of free sex began to pale because there was just so much of it, and I was actually looking forward to starting work. But the week before I was due to leave Thailand, I found myself browsing through the Craigslist website, looking for something, or someone, to do. I checked the Women Seeking Men page but didn't see anything there that I fancied, so I went through the Erotica section, but they were all pay-for-play birds. If I wanted to pay for sex I'd rather pick up a dancer from Soi Cowboy.

Then I went to Casual Encounters and, bingo, there it was: 'Fancy A Gang Bang In Pattaya?' I wasn't sure whether the offer was giving or receiving, but I clicked on it anyway. The first thing I saw was a picture of a fit Asian bird, probably Thai, with great tits and hair down to her waist and a black strip across her eyes and nose so you couldn't see her face, but the body was out of this world. Fit as a butcher's dog, as my dear old dad used to say. It was hard to judge her age. She wasn't a teenager, but she could have been anywhere between twenty and thirty and didn't look as if she'd had kids.

She was lying on a bed, her back against the headboard and her legs akimbo, her modesty shielded by a small white towel that wasn't much bigger than a flannel. It was her husband that had placed the advert. He said that his wife had a fantasy about being gang-raped and he wanted to film her being shagged by half a dozen or so blokes and that anyone interested in helping to realize his wife's dream should get in touch by email.

Alarm bells were ringing because I couldn't think that any man with a wife like that would want another man going near her, never mind inside her, but I opened up a fake Gmail account and sent him a message saying that I was interested and asking for more information.

He got back to me later that night with another photograph of his wife, fully naked this time, but with another black strip across her face, and a list of questions. Where was I from? What colour was I? How old was I? How much did I weigh? And he wanted a photograph, though I didn't have to show my face. I did, though, have to show my dick, which seemed a fair enough request considering what I was hoping to do with it.

So, I answered the questions fairly truthfully, though I did knock four years off my age and a couple of kilos off my weight. I took a photograph with the webcam of my laptop and made damn sure that I was holding my breath and attached that to the email. An hour later, he emailed me back with a mobile phone number and asked me to call him.

I went out and bought a new AIS SIM card and tapped out his number. He was English, quite well spoken, bit of a Hooray Henry, I thought. He said his name was Bill and I said I was Jonah. My private joke; I said I was hoping to have a whale of a time, but he didn't seem to get my attempt at humour.

He had more questions for me, basically checking that I was who I said I was. I guess he didn't want a big sweaty African turning up to do the dirty with his nearest and dearest, which I guess under the circumstances was only natural. Eventually, it was my turn to ask a question, and to be honest I only had the one. Why?

It turned out that his wife had a bit of a past. She used to be a go-go dancer in one of the racier Nana Plaza bars and had been working for five years or so before he met her. In his mind, he was a white knight, riding to her rescue. I didn't see it that way, of course. Five years working in a go-go bar meant she'd probably been with more than a thousand men. Sloppy seconds didn't even come into it.

Anyway, she'd been the perfect wife for going on ten years apparently, a whore in the bedroom and a three-star chef in the kitchen. (Or maybe it was the other way around.) But recently she'd seemed unhappy, and after he'd got her drunk one night, it all came tumbling out. She missed the life, she missed having sex with strangers, and having just turned thirty-five, she was worried that men no longer wanted her. She didn't look thirty-five in the photographs, I have to say. I mentioned that to the guy and he agreed, saying his wife spent a lot of time in the gym and the beauty parlour.

The news of his wife's unhappiness hit Bill hard, but she explained that it wasn't about him, she loved him and never thought about being unfaithful, but she had this ache, this craving, that just wouldn't go away. He didn't say who first came up with the idea, but between them, they arrived at a solution. One night, with half a dozen guys. All strangers. For that one night, she could do whatever she wanted, as many times as she wanted, and her husband would video it so that she would always have the pictures to relive the memory.

It was the first time that he had mentioned a video and I said I didn't want to be filmed, but he said all the men would be wearing masks. He explained that his wife didn't want to see the faces of the men that she was having sex with, and also it meant that the men wouldn't be worried about being recognised, which suited me fine. Like I said, it's a small world. I asked him if our dicks would also be wearing masks, and he said that was up to the guys. Condoms would be optional because everyone would have to email him a medical certificate saying that they were free of all sexually transmitted diseases.

He asked me if I was still interested and I said I was, and that's when he gave me the details of where and when. It was that coming' Friday, which suited me just fine because on the Sunday I was flying to Singapore to start the new job. The next day, I went and paid a doctor five hundred baht for a medical certificate. The doctor didn't even bother asking for a blood test. I emailed a copy to Bill and he emailed me back to say that he looked forward to meeting me. I couldn't get over how polite he was, considering that I was going to be banging his wife and all.

Bill said that he'd booked a suite at the Sandy Spring Hotel in Pattaya, not far from the beach. On Friday, I paid a taxi driver one and a half thousand baht to drive me from Bangkok and had him drop me on the beach road. I told him that if he waited for me, he could drive me back in a few hours and he agreed to wait. He gave me a card with his mobile phone number, and I walked up Soi 13.

The event was due to kick off at eight o'clock in the evening and would end whenever Bill's wife said that she'd had enough. I was early, so I walked across Second Road and had a coffee and a sandwich in Starbucks as I watched elderly overweight sex tourists in vests and shorts waddle by with their bargirls. Pattaya is a funny old place, where every man is handsome and every girl is available—

at a price. It's also one of the suicide capitals of the world, where membership of the Pattaya Flying Club is achieved by taking a dive off a high-rise balcony, usually the result of a broken heart or an empty bank account and probably both.

At five to eight on the dot, I swallowed a Viagra tablet and wandered back down Soi 13 and into the hotel. I don't normally use chemicals to get an erection, but I was a bit apprehensive about performing in front of an audience. A uniformed busboy smiled and wished me a good evening. The pretty girls at reception nodded and smiled as I headed for the lift.

Riding up to the eighth floor, I took my mask out of my pocket. The first mask I'd bought was a rubber Bin Laden from a stall on Sukhumvit Road, not far from Nana Plaza, but it was bloody uncomfortable and I could hardly see out of it. I ended up buying a cowboy set from the toy department of the Emporium department store that included a small black mask to be worn when robbing stagecoaches. It was small and I had to loosen the elastic, but I figured that so long as it covered my eyes and nose it'd be fine. I slipped on the mask as I walked down the corridor and knocked on the door of Room 807.

The door was opened by a big man wearing a dark blue robe and a stocking over his head. I tried not to laugh as he offered me his hand and introduced himself. It was Bill. I shook his hand and he closed the door behind me. He was holding a clipboard and he ticked off my name. He had a huge beer gut, the pasty white flesh flecked with blue veins like a ripe Stilton, and knobbly knees that wouldn't have looked out of place on an elderly elephant. The fact that the stocking was squashing his features made it difficult to work out how old he was, but I guess he'd be in his fifties, early sixties maybe.

'Am I the first?' I asked, looking around. There was a sofa and a table and a large television but no other guests.

'You're the fifth; the others are in the bedroom,' he said, nodding at a door. 'This is where I meet and greet, and check that you're who you say you are. I have to be careful,' he said, in his plummy voice that made me think of afternoon cream teas and croquet on the lawn. 'I wouldn't want the wrong sort of person turning up.'

'Absolutely,' I said, though frankly I wasn't sure who the wrong sort of person would be when one was talking about gang-banging one's nearest and dearest.

He opened a door and took me through to the bedroom, where four men were standing around a cupboard laden with drinks. There was a short, stocky guy in a fake Lacoste shirt and baggy blue jeans wearing a black ski mask; a tall thin guy in a Chang Beer T-shirt and shorts wearing a rubber wolfman mask; a youngish guy in a tracksuit wearing a cardboard mask with a dog's face; and a guy in a Spiderman mask who had taken off his shirt to reveal the hairiest chest I'd ever seen. He looked like an ape, and his bow legs and close-cropped hair added to the effect. They all nodded at me.

They moved aside and Wolfman waved at the bottles of booze. 'Free drinks,' he said, nodding at Bill. 'Courtesy of our host.' I picked up a bottle of Tiger beer. Next to the booze there was a bowl filled with blue Viagra tablets, another filled with small white tablets that I guessed were Ecstasy, and several smaller bowls which could only have been cocaine. By the bed was a large bowl of condoms and two tubes of KY Jelly.

'We're waiting for one more, but I think we can get started,' said Bill, looking at his clipboard. 'Why don't you guys get ready.'

The guy in the ski mask took off his shirt and jeans. He wasn't wearing underwear and he already had a huge erection, which I figured was probably chemically-induced. The Hairy Guy took off his trousers to reveal legs that were just as hairy as his chest.

'I don't see your wife,' I said, popping the cap off my bottle of beer.

'She's in the bathroom,' he said.

'She bloody well better be,' said the guy in the ski mask. He had a Scottish accent. Glasgow maybe. As he turned to look at the bathroom door, I saw that he had a blue and white cross of St Andrew tattooed on his arse.

There was a knock on the door and Bill went through to the other room with his clipboard. I took off my shirt and trousers and hung them up in the wardrobe. I was wearing my Union Jack underwear, flying the flag. The Scotsman grinned and raised his beer bottle in salute. 'Nice,' he said. I hoped that he was talking about my boxer shorts and not my growing erection. I sipped my beer and tried to look as if it was the most natural thing in the world to be in a hotel bedroom with four naked men.

Bill returned with a short man in a linen suit and a pink shirt, his face hidden behind a fancy black mask that was studded with fake diamonds. 'Bon soir, so sorry I am late,' he said. He had a French accent and a large square chin with a dimple in the centre.

'Aye, better late than never,' growled the Scotsman, scratching his backside. 'Can we get started? Let the dogs see the rabbit?'

'Absolutely,' said Bill, putting his clipboard onto the cupboard.

'Just to recap the rules, gentlemen. Basically, everything goes unless my wife objects. Her word is final. If she wants to stop, you stop. If she doesn't want to do anything, you don't do it. She has a safe word. Two words, actually. High Heels. If she says "High Heels", then you know she's serious. I hope that's clear. If she says "Stop!" or "No", then you can ignore it, but if she follows it with "High Heels", then you have to stop. Are we all clear on that?' He picked up a small video recorder. It was a Sony, an HD version that stored its video on memory cards.

We all nodded. The Frenchman took off his clothes and then helped himself to a glass of wine. He was overweight and his skin was peppered with small brown moles, but he seemed totally at ease. I couldn't help but compare dicks. I'd have to say that I was about average, and that Dog Mask was the biggest by far. His member would have looked more at home on a medium-sized Shetland pony. The Scotsman's was the smallest, about the size, shape and colour of a small carrot. Not that size is important, right? I'm joking. Of course, size is important, and any girl who tells you different is lying.

Bill pointed at the bowl of condoms by the bed. 'I got all your medical certificates and I can assure you that my wife is clean, so it's up to you whether or not you use condoms.'

'Hate the things,' growled the Scotsman.

'Right,' said Bill, 'let's get the show on the road.' He went over to the bathroom, knocked on the door and opened it. 'We're ready for you now, honey,' he said.

She walked out of the bathroom. I'd been worried that perhaps the photographs I'd seen had been Photoshopped, but if anything she was even sexier than in the pictures. She was tall for a Thai, but the stiletto heels made her look taller, with very white skin and long black hair that could have been used in a shampoo commercial, made even blacker by the contrast of the white towel robe she was wearing.

She had amazing cheekbones and as she slid off the robe I could see that her skin was totally unblemished, smooth and soft and white with absolutely no stretch marks or tramp stamps. She'd definitely never had kids, but I suspected that she'd had a bit of work on her face because her nose was bigger than you find on a Thai, even a Thai-Chinese, which she obviously was. She smiled at us and then bowed her head and *waied* us, putting her hands together as if in prayer. God, that was sexy, seeing as how she was totally naked, except for the shoes.

Her breasts were magnificent, large and full and proud and her stomach was as flat as a washboard. Bill hadn't lied about his wife regularly visiting the gym—you didn't get a body like that by accident.

She lay down on the bed, a sly smile on her face. The Scotsman made a whooping noise and jumped onto bed and thrust his groin at her face. She opened her mouth and took him straight away, clawing at his chest with her long nails, her eyes wide open. I swear her eyes were sparkling with pleasure as she worked on him, moaning softly.

The Frenchman growled like a dog and threw himself on the bed and pawed at her breasts. Bill had his video camera on and was filming away. I moved forward but the Hairy Guy stepped forward at the same time and we banged into each other. We both laughed nervously, I guess neither of us were used to touching another naked man.

'Age before beauty,' I said, waving for him to go first.

'Pearls before swine,' he said, stepping back. He had a Manchester accent and sounded a bit like Noel Gallagher from Oasis.

I grinned and got onto the bed. Bill's wife grinned and moved over to suck me, still holding on to the Scotsman's dick with her right hand. Her nails were long and painted blood red. I gasped as she took me into her mouth. She was good. My God, she was good.

It went on for hours. Hours and hours. Thank God for the Viagra. She was insatiable and so were we. She took us one at a time, two at a time, three at a time, and at one point she was on top of me while the Scotsman was in her arse, she was pleasuring Wolfman with her mouth while she had a hand on two other guys as if she was using ski poles. I don't know where the sixth guy was, but I know where Bill was, standing on the bed with his video camera, capturing it all for posterity.

There wasn't a single thing that she refused to do. Guys came inside her, over her, in her hair, up her arse, in her mouth. She begged for more, she wanted it harder, faster, longer. She mewed like a cat, yelped like a puppy in pain, and bellowed like an angry bull.

Pretty much every hour, Bill would stop and change the memory card in his camera and by midnight, there were four cards on the cupboard by the door.

We started taking breaks. The Scotsman kept going out on the balcony for a cigarette, the Frenchman kept taking showers, Wolfman did a line of cocaine once every thirty minutes, as regular as clockwork. I took another Viagra and four lines of coke and drank half a dozen beers. One of the guys, the one in the dog mask, gave up before midnight. He was having trouble breathing and said he was having chest pains. He'd taken two Viagra and it was a laugh seeing him trying to pull his trousers on over an erection the size of a policeman's truncheon. I don't remember him leaving because by then, I was doing Bill's wife from behind, pounding into her and grunting like a pig while the Scotsman slapped her backside and called her a whore and the Hairy Guy was thrusting in and out of her soft, wet mouth.

There was a lot of name-calling going on, I remember that. We were bastards, we were shits, we were rapists, we were swine. She was a bitch and a cow, a whore and worse.

She was bathed in sweat like a racehorse that had been ridden too hard, and by midnight her eyes were glazed and her mouth wide open, but she wouldn't stop, she wanted more and more and more and wouldn't let us stop even if we'd wanted to.

At one point, just after midnight, she went out onto the balcony and stood looking out over the sea as we took it in turns to screw her from behind. She wailed like a banshee all the time and I was sure that anyone walking down Beach Road must have been able to hear her. When the last guy had finished, I thought that would be the end of it, but she went back into the room and gave her husband a long, slow, blow job while he filmed her and then she lay on the bed again and started swearing at us, telling us all that we were babies and that if we were real men we'd rape her and make her beg for us to stop. We took her at her word and for the next hour, she was raped in every way that a man can rape a woman.

I left about two o'clock in the morning. I was exhausted, I was drained, and I was sore. By then it was just the Scotsman, the Frenchman and the Hairy Guy still at it, and she was taking everything they could throw at her.

No one said goodbye or God bless; in fact, no one even looked at me, they were too busy banging Bill's wife. On the way out, I helped myself to one of the memory cards. I know it was wrong, I know it was stealing, but I figured what the hell: I was one of the stars, so I deserved a memento. And I figured that Bill had more than enough video to look at over the coming years.

I took the mask off as I went into the lift, dropped it into a garbage bin on the street, and five minutes later, I was back in my taxi heading towards Bangkok, barely able to keep my eyes open.

* * *

The following week, I started my new job in Singapore. I worked long hours and put everything into the job, knowing that it's vital to give a good impression from day one. Other than the occasional visit to Orchard Towers—known locally as the Four Floors Of Whores—to pick up some paid-for company, I was practically a born-again virgin. After a week, I found myself checking Craigslist to see if Bill would tout his wife again. I used to watch the video, too, and it was almost as exciting as being there. In fact, it became a regular thing—I'd get home at midnight, after the London Stock Exchange had closed, open a bottle of beer, lie on the sofa and watch it on my big screen TV. I have to admit that I tried calling Bill's mobile number, but it had been disconnected and I sent him an email asking if he'd thought of arranging a rematch, but it went unanswered.

*   *   *

To be honest, and like I said, everything I'm telling you is God's own truth, I couldn't get that night out of my head. It was the best sex I've ever had, bar none. I don't know if it was the masks, the cocaine, the fact that I was there with strangers, or because Bill's wife was so enthusiastic, but nothing I'd ever done before or after came close. The memory, and the video, began to torment me, reminding me of what I'd never be able to have again. I realized that no matter what I did in the future, nothing would come close to the sexual experience that I'd had with Bill's wife. And then, two months after I'd started work in Singapore, they came back into my life, Bill and his wife, in a way that I'd never have expected.

The company arranged to fly over its top clients for a two-day presentation in Singapore—putting them up at the five-star Fullerton Hotel by the mouth of the Singapore River and taking them to the city's best bars and restaurants while promoting what we thought were the best investments in the region. We'd arranged company visits and interviews with government officials and economists and had several presentations and demonstrations. It's something most brokers do; the clients get an all expenses-paid holiday and we get to pitch sales to them face to face.

The presentation started on Thursday which gave our guests the option of extending their holidays over the weekend if they so wished—at our company's expense, of course. The guests arrived during the day and our first official get-together was in the evening in a suite at the Fullerton. Elegant waiters glided around with trays of canapés and vintage champagne flowed. I was munching on a piece of smoked salmon on a miniature bagel when I saw them.

I didn't recognise Bill at first because the last time I'd met him, he'd been wearing a stocking over his face, but there was no mistaking his drop-dead gorgeous wife. She was wearing a black dress, low cut to show off her amazing breasts and cut several inches above the knees to accentuate her fabulous legs. She had on stiletto heels and was carrying a tiny gold handbag; around her neck was a thin gold chain with a very large diamond and on her wrist was a diamond-studded Rolex. Pretty much every man turned to look at her as she walked into the room on Bill's arm. Bill was wearing a matching Rolex and a black Hugo Boss suit. He was in his late fifties and without the stocking, he was a good-looking guy in an Alec Baldwin sort of way, though with more grey at his temples.

He strode over to one of our company's top executives and shook his hand, then introduced his wife. She shook his hand, too, and smiled with her soft, warm mouth. I felt myself grow hard as the memories flooded back. Her standing on the balcony, moaning into the wind as we pounded into her from behind. I shivered.

'She's something, isn't she?'

I turned to see Robert Tam smiling at me. 'Bloody lovely,' I said. 'Who's the guy?'

'Bill Mayweather,' he said. 'He's based in Dubai. Runs an investment fund for one of the sheiks. He's on a percentage, and he's worth millions. Do you want an introduction?'

'You know him?'

'Known him for years,' said Robert. He sipped his champagne and smacked his lips. 'We don't do much business with him though. He has his favourites and it's bloody difficult to get into his inner circle.'

'I might be able to work some magic on him though,' I said. I could feel my heart pounding. Handled the right way, the memory card that I'd taken from the Sandy Spring Hotel could be just the magic I'd need to persuade good old Bill to let me into his inner circle.

'He's immune,' said Robert. 'Always cuts a deal in his favour, takes no prisoners, that's why the Arabs love him.'

I swirled my champagne around as I stared at Bill's wife's legs and her cute backside. I wanted to tell Robert what I'd done to her and what she'd done to me, but that was a secret best kept between me, her, and Bill. 'I think I might have some leverage,' I said.

'Leverage?' Robert chuckled. He gestured with his glass. 'Bill's wife, you mean?'

'What?' I turned to look at him, my mouth open.

'Forget about it, everybody knows about her,' said Robert.

'They do?'

Robert nodded. 'Everybody knows, but nobody says anything. It's up to him, right? You make your own bed and you lie in it.'

I nodded, but my mind was whirling. How the hell did everyone know what had happened at the Sandy Spring Hotel? 'I guess so,' I said.

'Beautiful. Sexy as hell.'

'Thai,' I said. 'Thai-Chinese, probably.'

'All the best ones are,' he said, and I frowned, not understanding what he meant. He didn't notice my confusion and carried on talking as he looked her up and down. 'She used to work at Casanova's, the bar in Nana Plaza,' he said. 'One of the star turns, apparently.'

I almost choked. I knew the Casanova Bar. Knew of it, but had never been outside. The aggressive ladyboys with too much make-up and enormous silicon breasts meant that I tended to hurry by with my eyes averted. I'd never been a fan of ladyboys.

'Bill met her about ten years ago, before she'd had anything done. Basically, she was a guy with long hair back then.' Robert chuckled and looked around to make sure that no one else could hear him. 'He paid for the lot. Hormones for the skin, new breasts, plastic surgery on the face, collagen in the lips, and then finally ...' He made a snipping gesture with his right hand. 'She had the chop. Or he had the chop. Had it done in Switzerland by one of the top surgeons in the world. Apparently it's as good as the real thing, except for the old-lubrication problem.'

Lubrication? That's right; that would explain the KY Jelly by the bed.

'Are you okay?' asked Robert, gripping my shoulder. 'You look like you've seen a ghost.'

I shook my head. 'I'm fine,' I said.

'Anyway, there's no leverage there. Everybody knows. It's the secret that everyone knows and no one mentions. You make your own choices in life, don't you?'

I nodded. Yes, that's absolutely what we do. We make choices and we live with them.

'She's fit though, isn't she?' I nodded. Yes, she was fit.

'I'm not sure I could ever give her one, though,' said Robert, slapping me on the back. 'Not knowing that she used to be a guy. What about you? Could you give her one?'

'Nah,' I said. 'Never happen.'

'There are those that say no one screws like a ladyboy,' said Robert, gripping my shoulder. 'They say no one knows what a guy wants better than another guy. What do you think? Think that's true?'

'Nah, I like girls,' I said, but I was finding it difficult to speak. My mouth had gone bone dry. I drained my glass, but my throat was still dry.

'Don't we all?' said Robert. 'Still, each to his own. If Bill's happy, that's all that matters. Whatever rocks your boat, right?'

'Right.' And with that, Robert slapped me on the back again and went over to talk to Bill and his wife.

So, that was that. Any thoughts of using the memory card as leverage against Bill went straight out of the window. I was confused, though. Damn confused. The only thing that I could think about just then was that the most intense sexual experience of my life had been in a room with eight other men.

And here's the thing, the thing that worries me most: I didn't care. I really didn't care. The fact that Bill's wife was a transsexual didn't worry me one little bit. I still watched and rewatched the video. I still visited the Craigslist website hoping that Bill would arrange a rematch. I still relived that night in the Sandy Spring Hotel—every moment, every position, every orgasm.

I spent so much time daydreaming that my work went downhill and Robert had me in for a chat to say that unless things turned around, he'd have to let me go. I didn't give him the chance. I applied for a job with a broker in Bangkok and got it. It was half the salary and no accommodation allowance, but that didn't matter. I just wanted to be in Bangkok, just in case Bill's wife ever wanted to relive the experience.

And that's why I'm here, sitting in Business Class and drinking this very reasonable champagne, heading back to the Land Of Smiles. I'm sure that one day, sooner or later, Bill's wife is going to want to do it again, and when she does, I want to be there. And if she doesn't ...well, maybe I'll swing by Casanova's and see what's on offer there.

Stephen Leather is the author of more than twenty novels, including *Private Dancer* and *Confessions of a Bangkok Private Eye* published by Monsoon Books in Singapore, and the Dan 'Spider' Shepherd series and the Jack Nightingale series, both published by Hodder and Stoughton in the United Kingdom. You can find more details of his work at *www.stephenleather.com.*

Less Than A Day

John Burdett

1.

Just because I'm going to Bangkok, doesn't mean I'll ...

Since he was talking to himself Fred didn't need to complete the sentence. His internal dialogue consisted mostly of such snippets: *loath the exploitation of women ... anyway have a relationship ... whatever that means ... at least think I do ... giving it an effin good try anyway.*

He was in a business lounge at Heathrow. To prove his point to himself, he fished out his mobile and dialled a number he knew by heart, but had not yet assigned to autodial. It rang until her voice began reciting her automatic reply. She had gone out of her way to be charming to callers both known and anonymous: *do, do, try me again later, I'm in a meeting just now ...* Except she wasn't in a meeting. It was quite early Sunday morning. Fred had to leave the UK on his day off in order to start work on his assignment Monday night, in order to get back to the UK, the office and *her* before the end of the week.

He knew it would be quite a squeeze, but no reason why he

couldn't manage. It was a straightforward story with a nice dark theme: middle-aged Englishman falls for Thai bargirl, buys a house in the country and a car for them, both of which he puts in her name: a magnificent two story Spanish-Asian fusion job with double car port and a Toyota 4x4. Then she dumps him. Legally both house and car are hers: he no longer has the right to live in his own home. It turns out she had a boyfriend her own age just down the road in her village. Then, if that were not tragic enough, the poor guy— his name was James Conway, aged fifty-five—gets shot in the head when walking home from the local bar one night.

Cruelty and murder were like porn: readers were automatically hooked. And there were enough middle-aged Englishmen living with ex-bargirls, both in the UK and overseas—perhaps a little paranoid about their relationships—for the story to improve subscription numbers.

That's why Fred's editor wanted him to chase it. Fred was heterosexual and under thirty, which pretty much made him the obvious choice. More: Fred had spent a year in Paris, so he was cosmopolitan; it had to be him. Of course, the big-time media had broken the story already, for about a nanosecond. As far as Fred's editor knew, no one was doing it in depth though. Except Fred, who would end up spending a whole week of his life on it, if you took the travel time into account.

'While you're there, see if you can dig up a few more yarns, the kind we can store for a while ... You know the sort of thing.'

Of course, Fred didn't know the sort of thing, and neither did his editor, but any old dark stories would do. Everybody said what a lucky chap he was, whilst secretly relieved they didn't have to go themselves: such a long trip, no friends out there, not as if he was going to a beach or anything truly exotic, the murder happened in deep country, a place called Isaan. And, let's face it, Thailand, for all its charm, was Third World, even though it wasn't PC to say so.

The fact that *she*—her name was Penny, but since he could not claim a romantic connection with any other woman, she appeared in his inner life as simply *she* or *her*—was not answering her phone caused a mild panic, a fluttering somewhere in his stomach. She knew he was at the airport, waiting for a plane that would take him away for a week right at the beginning of their ... whatever it was. He sent a text message with a much jollier tone than he felt: *Off to the wild East in about an hour, missing you already.*

He hesitated before pressing *Send*. On an emotional level the message expressed a deeper commitment than either had agreed to so far. All they'd done was get drunk and stoned and have sex, but the sex had been *so* good—they'd discussed it in real time over their mobiles the next day—that a re-run was certainly on the cards. Apart from that, their budding romance was conducted electronically: texts for short *Hi theres*, emails for longer, more structured sentences: *God your tits are just, well, out of this world, I don't just mean size, I mean everything, shape, firmness, proportion ... I was thinking of them at five o'clock this morning ... Sorry if this is too, you know ...*

Don't worry, Sugarplum, I think we both had the bang of our lives, didn't we? I know I did. I never would have guessed you were so big ... I woke up thinking about your bits too ...

Love? Hardly, whatever *that* was, but a beginning of something that had a chance of survival? Maybe. He was just sick and tired of the endless chase for emotional stability, but you couldn't fess up to that, especially not *at the beginning*. Nobody could afford to be someone else's crutch & crotch for life, not if you wanted to stay in the race, keep upwardly mobile, pay off the mortgage on your studio flat, think about buying a decent car—finally. He pressed *Send*, anyway, wondering if he was being uncool. To be honest, he hoped for a reply within the minute. She took forty and, to his own astonishment, the wait caused him to come out in a cold sweat and an inner voice started saying nasty, vengeful things about *her*, until his phone whooshed—it was his main life style decision that he preferred whooshes to bleeps : *Have a great trip, see you when you get back, you lucky dog.*

No *missing you too*, he noted. And who was she with at nine o'clock on a Sunday that she couldn't answer her phone or reply to a text message without making him wait more than half an hour? He felt the onset of depression. Then his phone whooshed again: *I'm gonna miss you too, Sugarplum.*

Now he felt like a million. The odd thing, of course, was that their relationship—if they had one—would not actually change at all. Neither had had time to meet again for the action replay, and they could text and email just the same while he was in Thailand as when they were ten miles apart in London. So, in terms of cyberspace , nothing was going to change over the next week. Was it?

Fred took out a book he'd bought the day before by some expat Brit who'd made a name for himself writing *noir* novels about Bangkok bargirls. He speed read it, skipping all the poverty-and-preaching stuff, grabbing what he needed. The main point was that Bangkok bargirls almost all came from this Isaan place, which was in the Northeast. He figured a smart move would be to spend Monday night doing the bars in Bangkok and learning about Isaan, so he'd have all the background he needed without having to schlep all over the countryside in a hire car. If he had any talent at all, he told himself, it was for finding the quickest smartest way to the guts of his stories.

2.

Fred wasn't sure of anything except it was Tuesday and there was a body in the bed next to him. When he adjusted his mobile to Thai time, it was still Tuesday, but much later in the day and the brown girl was turned away from him. He stood up to walk around the bed and look at her. His first reaction was to congratulate himself on his good taste. This was a truly beautiful woman, with high cheek bones and an elegant gauntness, full sweet lips. From the shape of the bed clothes, the rest of her was pretty well put together, too. When she smiled he felt even more pleased with himself.

'Hi. I'm Lalita.'

'Right,' Fred said. 'I'm Fred.'

'I know. I wasn't drunk last night.'

Fred nodded thoughtfully. 'Would you mind telling me what happened?'

'You got drunk and kept telling me how beautiful I was. You paid my bar fine, so I had to look after you. You were going to ring the bell, but I stopped you.' Her English was almost perfect, with a mid-Atlantic accent.

'Bell?'

'Every bar has a bell. If you ring it you have to buy everyone a drink. There were about fifty people there. I saved you about twenty thousand baht.'

He made the calculation. A thousand quid? Jesus. 'Thanks.'

She smiled again. 'But you were too drunk to get it up. You want to do it now?'

Fred blinked. 'You want to?'

'I don't care. I want to get paid, but I'm not a beggar. So?'

He took a step forward, which brought him to the edge of the bed. He was naked except for his shorts, which she pulled down enough to expose his member. She rose to sit cross-legged on the bed, in T-shirt and panties. He watched her cup one hand under his testicles and, with the other, slowly, expertly, and tenderly produce an erection. She made sure it was good and firm before putting it in her mouth. After a minute or so she took it out again. 'You want to come like this, or you want to fuck me?'

'I don't know,' Fred said, still half drunk, 'to tell the truth I think ...' He put out a hand to steady himself on her thin shoulder. A spasm.

Now his sperm was all over her tiny brown hand. She shook it as if she was shaking off a cobweb. Suddenly anxious to save her from indignity—beauty had that effect on him—he grabbed a box of Kleenex that was on the bedside table and handed it to her. She first cleaned him, then her hand.

'Well,' Fred said, still leaning on her shoulder and feeling dizzy.

She looked into his eyes. 'You want me to stick around so you can do it properly? Or are you always like this? Are you alcoholic?'

'How much d'you want?'

'Two thousand baht, same as if you fucked me. That's because I stayed the night with you.'

Two thousand baht: that was less than he'd spent on champagne on that one and only night with Penny. And it wasn't even a full night. He'd had to get in his car at a freezing 3 am because she couldn't sleep with someone else in the bed with her. 'I understand.'

'So?'

'We don't have to do it. Just stick around for an hour or so, I'd like to ask you some questions.'

'Again?'

'Was I that drunk? Did someone spike my drink?'

'Why would anyone do that? Have you been looking at one of those websites?'

A pause while he looked around the room. 'Maybe I do have a drink problem,' he said, mostly to himself. He remembered, now, how wired he was when he hit the bars. When wired, he drank. It went with the job.

In London, if you wanted people to talk, you bought them drinks. No one likes to drink alone, so you drink with them.

He'd never had such a complete memory blackout before though. Maybe it was the jetlag. He shrugged. 'Did I ask you about Isaan?'

'Yes.'

'And about that case?'

'The English guy who got shot to death? Yes.'

Fred pulled his shorts back up and sat next to her on the bed. There was something deeply troubling about this situation that he could not quite put his finger on. She was so friendly, chummy even, like they were old pals. It wasn't right to feel this relaxed with a stranger, a whore, in a country he'd been in for less than a day. Culture shock: he couldn't think of anything so thoroughly un-British. Where was the paranoia on both sides, the mutual contempt between prostitute and client, the guilt, the nausea? And how was it he was starting to feel horny after he'd just come? That hadn't happened to him since he was sixteen. He slipped a hand up her back under the T-shirt, then round to her breasts. Full, young, firm. He felt that hand again, working the outside of his shorts this time. He groaned with a sense of foreboding: *If this is as good as it looks where the eff have I been all my life?*

She slipped out of her T-shirt and panties, pushed him back on the bed so she could pull his shorts off, straddled him, worked on both his and her private parts until both their bodies were ready for fluid exchange, then reached behind him to find a condom, which she spread wide and slipped on. Now she eased him inside her. He couldn't believe it. Exactly five and a half thrusts and he was jerking uncontrollably again. She eased herself off of him, carefully removed the clotted condom, cleaned him again, took the condom to the bathroom, returned, naked, with another of those incredible smiles.

'Why are you crying, Fred?'

'I don't know,' Fred said.

'Don't know?'

'I think it might be because you've just made a fantasy come true, and that scares the living shit out of me.'

She blinked. He'd lost her in his culture shock. 'You need an interpreter when you go to Isaan?'

'Oh Christ yes,' Fred said, wiping his cheeks with a Kleenex.

'You'll have to pay my bar fine for as long as it takes.'

'Whatever,' Fred said, 'It's all on expenses.'

'Really?'

'I mean the interpreting, not the sex.'

She pulled on her T-shirt and panties and fished a mobile out of a handbag. She spoke rapidly in Thai, then closed the phone. 'You have to pay for a week, in advance. Give me the money so I can take it to the *mamasan* now. Or is a week too long?'

'How about we make it a year?' Fred said.

That made her laugh, an old-fashioned belly laugh like his granny used to have. In London they didn't laugh like that anymore.

'Eleven hours,' Fred muttered, looking at his cellphone.

3.

'D'you love me?' Fred said.

'Of course not,' Lalita said, 'I hardly know you.' She smiled. 'I love your money, though, and the way you're being so nice to me.'

'Aren't your other customers nice to you?'

She thought about it. 'English are mostly nice, but they drink too much and get hysterical. Germans are too harsh, but okay ... Japanese are weird but have tons of dough and— '

'Stop,' Fred said. 'D'you always have to be so honest?'

'Why? In your country you're not honest?'

'No. We lie all the time.'

'About what?'

'Compared to you, everything.' He let a beat pass, then added:

135

'I love *you*, though.'

'Liar.'

He'd let her drive the hire car. She explained that there were surely going to be cops to bribe sooner or later, and the bribes would be lower if she was at the wheel, rather than a *farang*.

'So, are we near the village where that bloke was murdered?'

'Not so far, but we're not going there. We're going to the village next door.'

'Why?'

She frowned as if he were retarded. 'Because at the village where he was murdered they won't tell us anything. They'll be afraid of losing face. At the village next door, they'll tell us everything so the village where he was murdered will lose face.'

'Got it,' Fred said.

Paddy fields the dense green of pool tables, ramshackle wood houses on stilts. The roads were almost deserted except for a few pick-up trucks with farm labourers in the back, their faces swathed in cloths and T-shirts against the sun and dust. Lalita reached across to his crotch and squeezed.

'You feeling horny?' Fred said.

'No. I almost never feel horny. I'm just taking care of you. I'm at work, don't forget.'

'You're going to kill me with being so honest.'

'You want me to shut up?'

'Oh, no,' Fred said. 'I want to die this way. Please, keep up the torture.'

She laughed that laugh. He'd noticed that whenever death was mentioned, it made her laugh. She'd told him it was from Buddhism: death was a kind of joke, once you got the message. Then she asked in a humble tone he'd not heard from her before if he minded if they stopped off for half an hour at her own village, which was on the way. Her grandmother was dying.

'Sure,' Fred said, 'I have a thing about my own granny.'

'You see her much?'

'She's dead.'

Lalita laughed.

He waited while she ran inside a small shack on stilts. Two kids played in a mud patch, an alcoholic grandfather sat and stared at him as if he wanted to kill him, an exhausted middle-aged woman in a worn grey sarong put her hands together to greet him. When Lalita ran out of the shack again, she introduced her mother. Then they were off.

'Whose are the kids?' Fred said.

'My sister's, but she did her head in with meths and they locked her away in the funny farm.' She shrugged. 'Someone has to give them a chance.' She didn't say it, she didn't need to: that bunch of losers in the shack was the reason she sold her body. *And they're not even her kids*, Fred thought, with an incredulity that was hard to live with.

4.

Fred said: 'How come you speak such good English, Lalita?'

His memory of the night before had recovered somewhat. He

recalled that apart from her good looks and great body, Lalita had stood out from all the other girls for her mastery of the language—and superior intelligence. It was entirely possible that she had chosen him rather than the other way around. She could be playing him like a penny whistle—which didn't bother him at all. He was enjoying the tune.

'I had a sponsor,' Lalita said, 'A *sugar daddy* as you call it. He was an engineer. English, but spent all his working life in the United States. That's why I speak the way I do. I lived with him. I mean, he had a big apartment in Bangkok and I lived there full-time. He travelled all over Southeast Asia on his engineering assignments. When he was home, we spoke English, when he was away I studied English—there was nothing else to do. It was part of my contract with him that I wouldn't take on other customers. I was only nineteen and my brain worked good.'

'What happened?'

Fred saw something strange in Lalita's face. He was not used to Thai features. He couldn't tell if a memory was causing her extreme pain—or something else.

She inhaled heavily. 'You really want to know what happened?'

'Yes.'

'Well, see, he would often be away for months at a time, sometimes six months, and he said his work didn't allow him to fool around with other women, so when he returned he was pretty horny. I wasn't enough for him on the first nights back, so I had to arrange a threesome. I was fine with that, because it was always fun and relieved the pressure on me. I would find a girl in one of the bars which had upstairs rooms and I would have to tell her in advance what he wanted, otherwise everyone could get all tangled up and lose the moment. He liked to fuck me doggy-style while she lay underneath pointing the other way so she could lick his balls and his ass.

'Now, to understand you have to know that while she was licking him he couldn't move without interrupting her work and bumping her on the nose, so he would stay still and I would move in and out.' She gave Fred a glance.

'Okay,' Fred said.

'So, one night it was all going perfectly. She kept on licking and I kept on thrusting with my butt, except that it went on for a long time and he wasn't groaning the way he usually did. At first, I didn't think anything usual was happening because he'd taken a whole Viagra and was going to be stiff for hours anyway.

'I guess we went on like that for maybe twenty-five minutes or more, waiting for a tell-tale groan or two, and I was starting to get dry and her tongue was starting to ache before we realized he was having a seizure and couldn't speak or move. So we both got out from under him, but by the time we laid him on his back he was dead. You could say we'd been having sex with a corpse.'

Startled, Fred stared at her. She was biting her tongue.

'We ran to tell the *mamasan*, who came up and said we had to drag him downstairs because she wasn't supposed to rent out rooms for sex and she wanted it to look straight before she called the cops. But before we dragged him downstairs, she had to close the bar. So we did and the cops came and called for an ambulance and we were left with just us girls in the bar.'

'Okay.'

Lalita's face was trembling uncontrollably. For a moment, Fred wondered if she, too, was not having a seizure. Tears started to stream down her face. Now she exploded.

'It was just so fucking funny—all we girls and the *mamasan* had a party all night and drank the bar dry. I mean, out-of-control funny and shocking, too, which made it even more funny.' She struggled to keep her hands on the wheel in the grip of a prolonged belly laugh that caused her breasts to bounce and her shoulders to shudder.

Fred gave her a few beats to recover. 'You weren't sad in any way?'

She caught her breath. 'Why? He was a nice guy and had a great life, but how long was he going to live anyway? He was already fifty-six. Better to go that way than in a wheelchair sucking on an oxygen tube.'

'Right,' Fred said, scratching his jaw.

She flashed him a glance. 'What's the matter?'

Fred wasn't entirely sure what the matter was. After a couple of minutes he said: 'I think I'm the opposite to that bloke. I think I've been dead all my life and I'm only just coming alive.'

'Maybe you're not so different,' Lalita said. 'He told me he played it straight until he was thirty, followed all the rules and married a *farang* feminist who took everything including the kids. That's when he saw the light.'

5.

'Of course, *Khun* James Conway got shot: he was an asshole,' the village headman said; at least, that was how Lalita interpreted his words—freely, Fred suspected. 'He treated his wife like some kind of slave and he was in a bad mood all the time, always complaining. He had a drink problem and spent all his time at the bar. In the end they didn't bother with *cans* of beer, they served him with packs of twelve.

'He was an arrogant shit, always yelling and criticizing Thailand. How that guy could bitch! It was amazing. He could moan for hours about a cockroach crawling across the floor, on and on and on like a buffalo chewing grass. We know we're poor and low class, but he didn't have to rub it in like that. And he was a know-all—told the villagers how to do everything, even told them how to live. And he was insulting about Buddhism.

'His wife did her best for the first year. She was very patient and she's young, only twenty-three now. Then she lost interest and went over to her uncle's place to socialize with her cousins.'

'She was unfaithful to him?' Fred asked.

'Of course not. She married him properly, village ceremony and the legal thing, both. Isaan women take that very seriously.'

'Do you know who shot him?'

The headman shrugged. 'Who would know such a thing? Anyone in that village would have shot him if they had the chance. They're quite primitive over there. Maybe someone just happened to have a gun when they saw him walking down the street—a kind of accident, if you see what I mean. Or maybe they drew lots.'

'What about the police investigation?'

The headman stared at Lalita and made a gesture toward Fred, then snapped out something in Thai: 'What investigation? Why would the police be interested? He was going to get himself killed wherever he went, and if someone's caught, they will bribe the police chief, so nobody will ever know who did it.'

Now both the headman and Lalita looked at Fred as if he were retarded. Fred didn't know why he was enjoying it. 'So he just got wasted for being an asshole?' Fred summed up.

'Right,' Lalita said, not bothering to refer to the headman.

6.

Fred did his professional duty and checked out the village where James Conway was shot, even visited the Sino-Alicante monstrosity the Englishman had built with its garish green tiles, blinding white walls and stark blue swimming pool.

They went on to the bar where he drank, the spot where he died. Nobody in the village would talk, not even to the point of saying where Conway's widow was now.

But Fred knew he was only going through the motions. When his mobile whooshed with a message from Penny (*Where are you Sugarplum? Look, I know I've been a bit standoffish, but I'm coming round, give me time and I'm yours, okay? Just don't go needy on me—you have that needy thing, frankly, and it scares me—I have to be all about me right now, that's all, nothing else in the way*), he muttered something obscene and deleted the message.

He'd already written the Conway story in his head. He was clever with words and would make the investigative reporting good and *noir*, but the message was plain for anyone with a brain: *Jerk had it coming*. He also knew how he would end the report: *By the way, I resign*. Then he walked with Lalita through the village to a meadow that sloped gently down to a bubbling brook.

'Any land for sale here?' Fred said.

'Plenty. If you're serious, we should go back to Bangkok, then I'll return alone to negotiate—you will get a better price that way.'

'All in your name, of course?'

'It's the only way.'

'I want the house in wood on stilts. What about the car?'

'It will be mine too; you can't register in your name with a tourist visa. Don't do it if you're scared.'

'I'm not,' Fred said. 'But if I turn into an asshole, don't shoot me yourself. Let someone else do it. I wouldn't want you to do jail time for a selfish slob like me.' He thought he was making a joke, but his eyes teared. Lalita was silent and frowning for a long moment. 'You really can love me that quick?'

'Oh, yeah,' Fred said, then bellowed at the sky, 'HEAD OVER EFFIN HEELS, DARLING—as my granny used to say.'

He checked his mobile. Twenty three hours and forty-one minutes since he'd landed.

John Burdett was brought up in North London and attended Warwick University where he read English and American Literature. This left him largely unemployable until he re-trained as a barrister and went to work in Hong Kong. He made enough money there to retire early to write novels. To date he has published six novels, including the Bangkok series: *Bangkok 8*, *Bangkok Tattoo*, *Bangkok Haunts* and *The Godfather of Kathmandu*.

Good Morning, Bangkok

Andrew Penney

Savika. As Thai as the fragrant jasmine rice used each year in the Royal Ploughing Ceremony to ensure a good harvest. But—quite unmistakably—also a daughter of Mother India; the pink and bronze tones in her complexion telegraphed her Thai-Indian ancestry in a way which stiffened the cocks of a certain kind of Thai male with thoughts of Hindu gods making love in a sea of churning milk.

The General who was admiring her contours as she slept was one of those men. Although Savika's Indian features were softened by her Thai blood, the heft of her full breasts belonged to an *apsara*, one of those curvaceous Hindu sprites decorating temples all over Southeast Asia.

In the quiet street far below the sleek new studio apartment which the General used as a *garconnière*, street hawkers were setting up their noodle carts in the pre-dawn, and steady streams of Japanese cars were already threading themselves through the Bangkok roads in a routine which was designed to beat the dreaded rush hour jams of Krung Thep, the City of Angels.

* * *

It was so early in the morning that nearly every car in that thick flow of traffic had a sleeping child strapped into the back seat, an authentic Bangkok angel dreaming in his or her school uniform. The natives of Bangkok love to boast that their children eat, sleep, study, and are even born in cars; the city's traffic department has a squad of officers trained to nip through traffic jams on motorbikes and deliver babies in the gridlock.

Savika was sleeping so deeply that the General was able to use his cellphone to speak to his official driver without waking her. This was hardly surprising; the General was physically powerful, sexually experienced and was known to be a bold and demanding lover.

One of the national emblems of Thailand is the *garuda*, a fearsome and very virile male eagle which soared into Buddhist mythology via the Hindu culture that is at the root of so many things Thai. This includes the writing system, religious rituals, court etiquette, dance, music and art—even virtually every surname in the Kingdom. The Hindu God Krishna himself was said to have ridden into cosmic battles under a banner depicting this creature.

The General had swooped over—and against—Savika's supple young body like a *garuda*, taking his pleasure from the rich curves which felt so different from the smooth milky flesh of his main wife and his main concubine, who were both Sino-Thais of good birth, like himself.

He had spread her arms on the bed like wings and used his strength to press her wrists into the mattress as she moved her hips under him in that fierce Indian rhythm which they both enjoyed. The heavy breasts swelling above that narrow Indian waist had been crushed against his smooth chest during their lovemaking, and her heels had squeezed the firm muscles of his lower back when she wrapped her legs around his waist to pull him more deeply into her body.

*   .   *

The idea of making love with a dusky Indo-Thai woman represented erotic possibilities which were something like a drug for some Thai men. Savika herself took some very sharp pleasures from satisfying the General's tastes for Indian women, who were believed to be loose and uninhibited.

The erotic appeal of such women never failed to grip these Thai males, whether they were ethnic Thais, or a *luuk jeen* like the General, whose family had emigrated from China three centuries ago and risen to the very highest levels of Thai society—as courtiers, senior army officers, and titled merchants.

Indo-Thais had lived and prospered quietly in the Kingdom for centuries. It was a small community; fewer than 70,000 souls versus something like seven million Sino-Thais.

Like the Chinese, they had become utterly Thai, producing a caste of Thai-speaking businessmen and advisers. The chief Hindu priest of Thailand, who presided over royal rites, was Indian, and at least one Indo-Thai had served as a Privy Councillor.

*   *   *

Shortly before six in the morning, the General decided to wake his mistress for some brisk exercise before he headed for the office.

He bent his head between the thighs of the sleeping woman, and blew softly on the sensitive folds which were exposed because she was so relaxed that her thighs were slightly parted. When Savika's hips moved, her patron gripped her knees to part them even further and began to pull her out of her slumber by raking the lips of her *yoni* with his strong white teeth.

The General was fond of sleepy sex; he had a taste for watching women sleep and for taking them before they were awake enough to know whether they were ready to be penetrated by him. He loved feeling sleepy women tighten about his *lingam* in surprise as they began to realize what was happening to them.

None of his women were complaining. He knew that Savika, who happened to have the same name as a popular Indo-Thai TV actress, was particularly fond of being woken up for sex.

Yawning twice, she rubbed her eyes open and gazed at her patron, with eyes which were so large and dark that she looked like she was wearing eyeliner even without any makeup. The heavy gold dancer's anklets that she wore to feed the General's fantasies jingled lightly as he slid his lean body along hers, crushing her breasts once again, and pushed the heavy head of his very rigid *lingam* firmly past the warm, fragrant gates.

He wanted to devour his mistress; the dark and well-defined lips of her mouth became an early breakfast for him. He nipped and sucked at them and forced his tongue cleanly past her strong white teeth in exactly the way she liked, in a very deep embrace that pressed their tongues together and made his penis throb.

* * *

When the General penetrated his sleepy Indo-Thai *apsara*, he entered her in a sexual position which is known as the Bevel, his body fitting snugly against hers with every slow thrust, like the smooth bevels of a picture frame or a mirror. It was a classic position which permitted the man to enter a woman from the rear while she was lying on her back.

Kneeling astride her legs, he had grasped Savika's right ankle and pulled her leg right across her body until it was resting on his right thigh; this tilted her hips and exposed her smooth buttocks to him. He kept a firm grip on her ankle and began thrusting.

The General's young mistress gasped as she felt his *lingam* split her ripe body open and drive its thick head deep into her pussy with enough force to make the muscles of her anus clench and contract. She was dewy wet and deliciously tight. He enjoyed the low sounds which she was making as he took his time churning her hot inner sea in exactly the same way as the old Hindu gods might have churned the sea of cosmic milk with their bodies.

* * *

The General's cellphone beeped twice just as Savika began writhing under him from the force of her orgasm, and her inner muscles began squeezing his cock. It was a text message from the General's official driver, who had been circling the block. The General knew what the message said, but he merely grunted and continued to make love, allowing his mistress to take her time enjoying her little death.

Like many Thai men, the General had studied Tantric sex

techniques; this was a society where it was not considered shocking for men of his rank and wealth to juggle official concubines and mere mistresses, and love all of them well.

He used these techniques to control his ejaculation, withdrew from his woman and patted her on one rounded buttock; Savika's breasts were heaving and her smooth bronze skin was glowing from exertion. The mistress understood exactly what her patron wanted, and rose to a kneeling position on the bed. Tilting smoothly backwards, she arched her back like a bow to present herself to him, pillowing her head lazily on that thick glossy Indian hair, and on the hands which she kept crossed behind her neck.

And then she waited for the General to finish. His erection was dark with blood from his excitement, and bobbing aggressively as he moved between her thighs on his knees. Savika's crotch and her mound were completely smooth, in the Indian style which her patron appreciated very much; he paused to split that smoothness with his thumbs and make her moan before he reared over her again and re-penetrated her.

Several minutes later, the General's cellphone was beeping again, more insistently now, but nobody in the bedroom of that studio apartment was paying any attention; he was too busy riding his mistress, and he was also riding an orgasm which was so intense that he left marks on Savika's upper arms and printed her shoulder and her heavy breasts with the marks of his teeth.

After he was done ploughing that darkly succulent body and had spurted a decent amount of his seed into his mistress, the General rolled onto his back next to the young woman and put his hand on her thigh to feel the deep muscles of her legs trembling

149

from the effects of the very profound pleasures he had just inflicted upon her.

*   *   *

The lovers lay next to each other, panting. Savika rested one delicate hand on the rough but neat hairs of the General's groin, rubbing the backs of her fingers lazily over the base of the cock which had been so very angry and hungry, but was now very tired after all that exercise.

Her patron enjoyed the light cool weight of his young *mia noi*'s hand on his penis, which was still bobbing stubbornly as it took its usual time to soften. The General knew that he would not be able to climb into his official car any time soon; his penis had a mind of its own.

It was a full minute before Savika was composed enough to sit up and *wai* him graciously—bringing her hands as high as the middle of her forehead—and her patron had calmed down enough to greet her and wish her a pre-dawn good morning with an abbreviated but affectionate male *wai* of his own.

The young lady knew her patron well enough to bend her face down and use the tips of her fingers to touch his feet lightly, Indian-style, as if they were a husband and wife in India.

As is the case in Hindu India, touching the feet in Thailand is a very intimate gesture of submission and love, and the General's *lingam* began jerking to military attention again at her touch. Her rosy bottom, which was still completely naked, bobbed into his line of sight and sharpened his arousal.

The minor wife's Hindu curves always did that to him; he was severely tempted to flip her onto her belly and pin her down, so that he could feel her heart beating wildly as she submitted to him and waited—together with him—for him to become fully erect and take her yet again.

However, the beeps and chirps from the cellphone were becoming increasingly urgent, and the General decided, reluctantly, to wash himself and get into his dress whites for the long day of military duties ahead.

Savika watched her general languidly from the bed, without lifting a finger to help him; her eyes were half-closed under her very long eyelashes as she watched him bathe that hard body and dress himself.

She memorized the velvety heft of his penis in her hand as she bid him farewell by kissing him along the shaft. After her lover had let himself out of the tiny studio flat, she stretched herself out on the sheets like a contented oriental odalisque and dozed for a while, dreaming contentedly as another bright and muggy new day began dawning in Bangkok, the City of Angels.

Andrew Penney is the pseudonym of a very vanilla 42-year-old Singaporean who writes literary erotica.

Mad For It

Erich R. Sysak

So I'm in Phuket, Thailand, just a few weeks and I get a job teaching English. I need a clock to remind me to wake up. I want a big damn clock on the wall ticking like crazy. I go to Tesco in my tie and blue silk shirt and see an amazing Thai girl, about 27. Hair cut to the shoulders, wide mouth, a narrow waist that makes her hips and heavy breasts pull your eyes. Some women have this sexual power, like a love potion that people drink up. Karl Jung says it is a projection of the soul or *anima*. Walt Whitman says *steer for the deep waters only*.

Enter Goy and my first chance at exotic True Love. A long neck. Yearning in the face and dark eyes. A relaxed, nurturing vibe amplified by our struggle to communicate as she shows me how to work the clock. My arm brushes against her nipple as she winds up the mechanism. I'm happily swimming out to dark waters. A puff of her cream and cinnamon smell rises to my nostrils. But when I take the clock home, I just can't get it to work.

A few days later I come back, see her in jeans and a red blouse with SAME SAME on the curvy front. Somehow I get her in the mood and a short while later we're upstairs in the cafeteria eating

Japanese dumplings and fish sauce. She crosses her legs and laughs at me staring. Her toes are painted black. Even her feet are candy.

Her ex was a butterfly. She has a 3-year-old daughter back in Isaan. Phuket has all the decent jobs, but she misses the rubber tree farm back home. She's been working at Tesco five months and dealing with 12-hour days. She sends roughly one hundred dollars home each month. Half her salary.

She lives in a one-room apartment and eats cheap dinners. She's looking for the right man to save her. Show her the good life. And she's a swimmer. Her one day off: Sunday. She doesn't believe I'll take her to the beach, which is just as sweet as milk, so we find a shop and I pay for a white bikini. She puts it on at the back of the store and pulls the curtain back for three seconds to let me peek. Time slows. I see deep into her eyes. I see the dark circles of her nipples. I think red wine and French movies. Deserted beaches. Crazy, deep sex. TL.

Time goes on and life is paradise. Better than selling hard drives and meeting co-workers for after-dinner mimosas at Bennigans in America. I never think of the NFL or sitcoms or politics. She teaches me Thai. I teach her English. I feel deep, emotional thrumming in my stomach when we fuck.

*   *   *

Until she comes home one night a different woman. Wouldn't talk. Shrugs off my hands. Pouts like a little girl and it isn't sexy. There's a cold, white pallor to her face that just looks mean. Says she doesn't like work. The other girls gossip about her because she's with a *farang* and not married. She wants to quit work and take care of me. She wants money. Maybe move back to the farm and build a house in a rice field. Her parents need funds for everything: hospitals, food, booze, happiness. And then there's a dowry. A big one. I can't live without beaches and the ocean. I don't eat much rice.

And I didn't leave California with my pockets full of gold. About 20k in the bank and an old Taylor guitar on my back. I chew on *dowry* for a week or two, but she doesn't like delays. I came to Thailand because I can live in a bungalow near the beach, swim every day and eat mango, coconut and banana. Drink red wine. She locks herself in my bedroom and talks on her cellphone for hours. Comes out in a denim mini-skirt and heels and leaves me alone until midnight. I'm licking paint off the walls. She gets distant. Starts the going out thing a few times a week. I try to follow her once, but get lost in the mountains. I'm on a steep, dark incline. No streetlights. Weird sounds from the forest. A cool and ominous wind shakes the trees. I'm the only man on the planet. On the way down, I crash into a guard rail. Call her for help, but she doesn't answer. I know she's fucking around. But it feels like a way out. I didn't come to Thailand to be a wingman.

That night, I put her on the couch and yank at her twenty-dollar satin panties until she cries. I want proof. I want revenge. She buries her face in my shoulder. Tears soak through my shirt. I find her lips. My heart thumps. She sits on my lap and does this squeezing thing she can do with her vagina I don't understand and I let it go.

But it isn't back to normal. So I give her 500 dollars for her parents to do whatever. It makes her happy for a while. Pancakes and cheeseburgers fly out of our little kitchen. She buys a bus ticket home to deliver the money and quits her job. Which isn't exactly what I want, but the sex is so damn magical. She's so high on things, so full of trust that she brings me a piece of paper with 'You're a very special person. I don't want to lose contact with you' written on it in her handwriting. She says her friend got it as an SMS and she wants to know what it means. Yeah, right. I tell her what it means and wave goodbye as she climbs on the midnight bus to Korat.

I can't let it go. When she gets back, I demand to see her cellphone messages. She is good with the phone and when she opens the inbox, she deletes the first two before I have a chance to read them. Everything else is in Thai. I make her drive to DTAC and get the phone records. I read them standing in the mall and the names are all Thai. Maybe I was wrong. I feel bad. So I walk through the mall and see a travel agent. A lot of colorful brochures and long-tailed speed boats. I buy two tickets to the Phi Phi islands. Promise I will teach her to SCUBA dive. On the way back, she says, 'If you ever catch me lying, throw me out.' That really hits me. I was all wrong about her. She's the most beautiful woman I've ever known inside and out.

I buy two gold rings and carry them around in my pocket for a week. There is no place I can hide them in the house. She knows every spot. I walk around with my fingers in my pocket and dream.

On the night before the trip, she asks me when we have to leave. I say 7 a.m. She says she needs to go to the market before we take off, about 6. I ask her what she needs to buy. She says I don't know. Doesn't sound right at all. So in the morning, she's getting dressed and so am I. What are you doing, she asks. Going to the market, I say. She has a fit right there. Throws a coffee cup against the wall. Coffee splatters all over my art books. Glass on the floor. I think love is going to kill me. She goes alone and I just know what it is. I know.

When she's gone, I check my mail and the Internet saves me. She doesn't flush her cache from the night before because we were packing and eating and talking and I see where she was browsing: on this hook-up site called Tagged. Her profile just pops right up. She's got pictures I took of her in that damn bikini at the pool in the clubhouse. Says she likes a man who knows what he wants and hip-hop music. She's got friends. Lots of young European dudes with crew cuts. They look like football stars.

When you're 53, you know what's good for your soul. I've got a long history of great failure and great success. Western Digital paid me buckets to run the marketing. And I had a network of clients that locked me in. Took eleven years to go from copy writer to Big Dick. And when I got to the top, I didn't want to be there. I couldn't stop thinking about teaching music to kids or learning to sail, diving the reefs off the Catalina Islands. The trend went all the way back to Little League baseball. Best player on the team and then my mind turned to reefer and sci-fi novels which turned into a stint of guitar playing and modal jazz. I'm good for ten seconds at everything, and then it's over.

So I have my life-size epiphany in Stowe, Vermont, at this big marketing dinner paid for by Compaq with too much wine. I raise my hands to silence the table, then throw the question out. What's the absolute best thing in life? Everyone quickly agrees: true love.

It was all the proof I needed. Proof that the one thing I really wanted was TL. A deep, serious, honest connection with a fantastic woman was the one consistent theme of my life. And I admit Thai women had a certain appeal, a promise of youth and good odds. But I wasn't taking the exploitation angle seriously. Have you ever known one thing to be the way you hear it on the news or in the hallways at work? For me, never. I have to see things for myself.

But I'm not angry with Goy. What's the point? I just want to get rid of her now with as little conflict as possible and get on with my quest. I do love her, but I can't live with her. She's a devil. You know what I mean. We go to Phi Phi and I have the best three days of my life. Snorkeling in the glassy water. She takes me into the bushes behind the beach. Not a soul around except us and she fucks me as I sit on a pile of sand. She sucks my cock right there and her mouth is wet and shiny. She looks up at me with those tender eyes. And I lift her into my lap. Her cheeks feel damp on my fingers. I spread them and pull her close to my bulge. She groans and puts her hands on my shoulders. My cock juts out to find her hole. I feel her muscles squeeze in on me.

When she pulls my head down to suck her nipples, I see two Thai girls behind a coconut tree watching us. Goy looks, too, and she twitches somewhere deep inside. She looks back at me with a lewd smile on her face as I explode to the rhythm of a frantic popping sound coming from her groin. This is one woman it will be hard to forget.

*　*　*

On the last day, we're sitting in the restaurant. I'm drinking from a coconut. She's nibbling at sour mango. 'Goy,' I say, 'I will never be a rich man. You deserve a rich man who can take care of you and your family. I'll help you find this man. I can help you decide.' That's when I did become a wingman, but for a woman.

She confesses to wanting more on the financial end. It isn't her exactly, but her family that demands she marry someone wealthy to take care of them back in Isaan. An American woman just wouldn't think this way, but Thai women do. It's a different culture and you can't fight it. I wouldn't fight. I would use it.

When we get back, I look over her profile on Tagged. She shows me her friends, which ones she likes. We feel closer than ever now that the truth is out between us. I even read her messages from hundreds and hundreds of men. We're a desperate bunch. When I look at those messages to Goy I see us as conniving, weak, blathering wimps. It's just as ugly to me as it is to Goy and I imagine any other woman who reads such junk. First, I change her pictures. Not so sexy, more Bambi-esque. She really can hook you with those big eyes and smile. I re-write her profile. She wants a little danger in her life and she can't afford it on her own. She wants sunset cruises and a candy-apple red Honda Jazz. Are you the man for her?

The replies flood in. The liars are easy to spot. As we read the messages, she sits on my lap and I put my hands on her breasts and pull her big nipples. I get hard every time we do this. She tells me I have the biggest cock she's ever sucked. She can be so nasty. We read messages from doctors who can't spell simple words. CEOs who offer to send money right away. They offer plane tickets to Ireland, Norway, California, Geneva.

It's the moderate replies that I read with interest. The guys who want to know more and don't tout money. If you have it, you usually keep quiet about it or at least don't think about it too much.

I steer Goy to a retired, South African internist. Fifty-six. Says his wife died six years ago from cancer. He's retired to Phuket. Been living on the island one year. Knows just enough to want a cute Thai girl haunting his condominium hallways and bedrooms. Looks to be in good shape. Gray hair, but lots of it. A wedge-shaped haircut full of expensive gel. Big shoulders. Deck shoes. An honest smile. It is the smile that gets Goy. Says he looks kind. Whatever.

Goy agrees to meet him at the Natural Restaurant in Phuket Town. I drive her there and drop her off at the corner. She wobbles on her white heels up the sidewalk and I feel a terrible pain at the thought I'm making a crucial mistake I can't fix. Too many of these crucial mistakes and life kills you for sure or gives you psoriasis.

I'm up all night staring at the guy's profile on Tagged. I click the pictures over and over, looking for something and I don't know what. I walk up and down the living room floor with a hard-on and keep looking at my cellphone to see if I've missed a message. An hour is like five thousand years.

We didn't talk about sex. We didn't agree on any rules. It's about her. About her finding the right guy. Two-thirty, there's a little knock on the door. I'm wide awake. Savage in the eyes. She walks straight past me. I smell wine on her dress, the ocean at midnight. I call to her. I want the story. I want the details, but she shakes her head no and goes to the bedroom, shuts the door and locks it.

I go back to the computer right then. I know all of the buttons on Tagged and whip up my own profile. I post the picture from Phi Phi when I looked away from Goy in disgust as she happily snapped pics with the digital camera I bought for her. You can see the beach and the waves as a reflection in my Ray-Bans. I have my hands clenched in an expression of ultimate confidence. I find three more pics and load them up. Nothing sweet. They are manly, active pictures of the beach, a sailboat and me feeding rice to a neighbourhood stray dog. I have one pic with a Toyota 4x4 behind me and the door open. It looks like mine, but it isn't. I load that too.

Then I write a message. I cut and paste it and send it to almost fifty women who live on the island and grade at least a seven out of ten. It's a theory. The Wild 7. The tens are too beautiful and in Thailand, their beauty is a major asset. Perhaps all they have. And a lot of the other important qualities may not be there: humility, wit, sincerity. It's the slightly under-appreciated woman who has long-term possibilities. I want a girl who isn't a slave to her family. Who swims. Who doesn't worry if her skin gets too dark.

Then Goy appears from the bedroom. She sits in my lap and stares at my new Tagged profile on the computer screen. A wounded look appears in her little-girl eyes. I feel her satin panties against my thighs. She slides her arms around me. She lifts her brown nipple to my mouth. Her skin is soft and sends pulses of light through my body. I take her nipple in my mouth and it swells. I love the brown color, the rubbery feel of it in my teeth. Every part of her touches a part of me. She kisses me deeply and I regret it all as her hand pulls my throbbing cock out. I love her. She has it all. She pulls at it and I feel her long fingers curling around my head. We finally agree to stop torturing each other. She says she won't meet any more men on Tagged and I won't meet any women. She takes her soft fingers away just before I come. She'll get a job at one of the hotels and save money. I promise to help her more when I can.

She shows me an SMS from the doctor that proves they didn't have sex. The doctor says in the message that he wishes they had made love in the hot tub that night. Next time, he says. But there won't be a next time for him. I'm taking his next time and the next one too. TL isn't easy. But you have to hold on to it when you get it. She pulls her other leg over my head and lifts her ass. I guide her down onto my shaft and moan as I enter her. I am young again and will be inside of her forever.

But the truth is, we are living in a romantic dream that lasts only a few more weeks. Because she can't turn away from her own damaged search. And I know every good romance ends in death. It starts with a love potion. And the potion confuses everything that's real. The potion makes you do things that just don't make sense. Then you have a story and the story is full of lies and full of truth and there's no way to untangle it without a lot of difficulty. True Love. Whitman says, *I am mad for it to be in contact with me.*

Six months have passed, and Goy has what she wants now. She was on Tagged all along and that's no surprise. She lives in a mansion at Nai Harn Hill just above my favourite beach with a retired millionaire. He's Dutch. The owner of a shopping mall. He's overweight, hideous and shrewd. Goy hates him and gets everything she wants: a monthly salary, cooking school, that awful Honda Jazz and driving lessons. When I swim out to the bay, I can look back at the hill and just see the silver top of her water tower. I float in the bay and look up at it shining.

I've seen her a few times since she moved five months ago. We have sex sometimes and she cries after, but won't tell me why. When

I see her, I feel elated, and when we part, I feel relieved.

On my 54th birthday, I get an SMS from her. It says: I will always love only you.

And I will love only her, but she is gone from me and we will never have those beaches again. My madness is wanting her again, but knowing she is all wrong. What have I learned? Whitman was right about everything.

Erich R. Sysak grew up in Florida and New Orleans, but now lives in the northeast of Thailand. He works a small mango farm, reads and writes crime novels and teaches. His stories have appeared in *Oxford Magazine*, *storySouth*, the *Paumanok Review*, *42 Opus*, *Ducts* and *Pindeldyboz*. He has also written two crime novels: *Dog Catcher* and *Stage IV*, published by Monsoon Books. To learn more about Erich and his work, please visit *www.ersbooks.net*.

Painin

Brenton Rossow

I forgot to write Painin's phone number in my notebook. I could check it from one of her emails or go to the restaurant where she worked and ask one of her old workmates. I'd told Painin I would stay at the same bungalow but I didn't tell her the time I was arriving. It was stupid to think she'd be waiting for me. The man at the guesthouse said he hadn't seen her, so I pissed the colour of a hornbill's beak and headed towards her old restaurant. Painin's friend remembered me and giggled when she asked if I was Painin's darling, and tried to call *my baby*. The first time she didn't get through. The second time she got a hold of Painin as I was washing my hands in the bathroom.

I began to feel anxious. I adjusted my shirt, so I didn't look fat and positioned my chair so I could see Painin when she came into the restaurant. After a dry sandwich, I began leaning over the balustrade so I could see her as she drove up the street. I began to feel sleepy, stretched out on some cushions and fell asleep.

When I awoke an hour later, Painin still hadn't arrived. I went downstairs to speak to her friend with the mobile. After trying a few times and getting an engaged signal her friend got through and handed me the phone.

'Hello'

'Who's this?'

'It's Blinch from Thailand.'

'You no like me. Why you want see me?'

My heart sank. *What's she talking about? What's she playing at?*

'If I didn't like you, why would I come all the way to Vientiane? It's Blinch from Thailand. I was here six weeks ago. We sent each other emails. I miss you ... I want to see you.'

'I busy working now. I told you we finish already. I not want see you.'

'What? What are you talking about? You never said we were finished. Come and see me at the bungalow.'

'Okay. I come see you at 4 pm.'

What happened? My heart began fluttering all over the shop. *Why would she send me those emails saying she wanted to see me, then blow me off like a pencil shaving?*

I picked up my bag, smiled faintly at the girl in the restaurant who was blushing with embarrassment and began walking down the street. How sure I had been that our story would turn out the way I wanted. How confident I had been as I boarded the bus to Vientiane with photographs of Painin and Sai in the top pocket of my rucksack.

I decided to visit Uncle Mimi. Old Funky Lips wasted no time skinning up. We sat upstairs on his balcony, blowing smoke clouds into the street. He waited patiently, every so often nodding his head. Then, after I finished my story, he told me to forget Painin and find myself a new girl.

'Many girl,' he said, patting my shoulder. 'Lucky you no kid.'

I thanked Uncle Mimi, stepped out the doorway—heart hurting like crazy as the weed weaseled its way into my stream—and walked into the sunshine. In a vacant block across the street, I noticed some artists had strung paintings between the branches of a few spindly trees and fastened them together on a length of string. Cigarette at lip, beer in hand, I began to lose myself in the colours of jungle villages and the swirl of water lilies. I felt a warm hand on my shoulder. I turned and Painin was standing in front of me; toes hanging from high heels, miniskirt and a tight white midriff.

She looked up, smiled and took my hand.

'I was with my friend and I saw you look painting, so I come see.'

'I missed you, Painin. I don't understand why you're angry with me. I came all this way to be with you. What's going on?'

'You not help me when I ask you send money for motorbike. You not call. You not care.'

'Of course I care, but what could I do? I have to work six weeks before I get a holiday. It was impossible to come and see you right away.'

She raised her eyebrows and squeezed my hand. Looking down, I noticed she was carrying a plastic bag.

'What's that?'

'My new telephone, I just bought from market. I borrow money from friend.'

'How much was it?'

'Seven thousand. It have many song and photograph. It

very expensive.'

Something in the back of my mind registered things weren't okay, but I kept staring, hypnotized by her voluptuous lines.

'Where are we going?' I asked as she led me by the hand.

'I want go temple.'

'Here,' I said reaching into my rucksack. 'Here are some photos of you, Sai and my apartment in Thailand.'

She studied them, carefully lingering on the photo of my apartment, then stood on tippy toes and kissed me. It was a long slow kiss, full of absence and ecstasy. I held her by the hipbone and relished her warm tanned skin. She reached down and grabbed my balls, looked me in the eyes ... let go ... then continued walking. We walked past the temple and across the road to the grassy banks of The Kong.

Three of her friends appeared to be waiting outside a restaurant. It was obvious I'd be picking up the check. If I refused to go along with her plan, I'd embarrass Painin and she'd be furious.

One of Painin's friends—Noi the Freeloader—was slouched in a plastic chair, smiling in the sunshine. The sight of her made me queasy and flyblown.

On this occasion—quite like the first time I'd met her—she failed to acknowledge me. She quickly grabbed Painin by the elbow, turned her back and began devolving her plan.

From the moment I met Noi, I was aware she was young and foolish, but I was forced to tolerate her. The previous time we'd met she rolled up at a restaurant Painin and I were eating at as if it was her right to be there and my sole purpose was to pick up the bill. It made me sad to think Noi was poisoning Painin with her schemes.

Every time I looked at her, she sprayed a sickly green film across my skin.

'You okay, Noi?' I asked, best I could.

She raised her eyebrows as if to say *Fuck off loser—I'm just here for the freebee,*ducked her head to avoid a pot plant and catapulted herself inside. Painin's other friends—two tall, tanned sisters whom I'd never met—appeared friendly. We sat down at a table—Painin and Noi ordering food—and before I knew it, a banquet appeared. As the older sister and I spoke, she gave me the feeling she felt sorry for me, politely refilling my glass while Noi and Painin exchanged glances.

'I'm going home tomorrow. My father sick. I need you give money.'

I just played along, but what I was really thinking was *Come on, Painin ... you're smarter than that.*

'Really ... you're going back to your village? How about I come with you so I can meet your family?'

Noi nearly choked on a piece of pork that was swirling about her mouth and rushed to the toilet. The two sisters looked into their drinks, slightly ashamed. I took Painin by the hand and led her into the sunshine.

What the fuck was I doing? Her shoes were too small and her toes hung out like monkey digits. Her skirt was too tight and when she sat, a few flab rolls appeared. But they weren't ugly flab rolls and her toes appeared primal and sexual. She'd run a slight wave through her hair and sported a new pair of goofy aviators. No matter how much shite she spun, no matter how many financial demands, I couldn't help being attracted to her. I kept telling myself she was a good girl at heart and she could change if I got her away from sneaky friends like Noi the Freeloader.

We walked back to the restaurant and said goodbye to Noi and the two tall tanned sisters. Her motorbike was parked next to a security guard and it looked shinier than the last time I'd seen it. We skidded along the gravel, slowly hiccupped through the streets and made our way back to my bungalow.

Painin threw herself on the bed with her knees up and her peach-coloured knickers showing, fanning her legs like the wings of a butterfly. I kissed a kneecap and stepped into the shower to wash the journey's sweat from my skin.

When I returned, she had her knickers off and was smiling. I leapt on the bed and began kissing her neck—soft sweet stamens of a spider orchid—then dragged my tongue to the outskirts of her belly and got lost in the trees. She laid back, smiling—devil in the eyes, lips quivering—and fiddled with her new phone. A song played and it was modern and slick—not exactly romantic—but full of the latest guitar sounds with a heavy bass beat.

I lost consciousness. My spirit hovered. I disappeared inside the vines of a deserted temple and knelt at the dripping feet of an ancient mollusk. I collapsed beside her as orange swamp gas exuded from the pores of my skin. I was born again: immortal—everything perfect—reality a ghost without a name.

Painin stood, smiled and walked into the bathroom, lathered herself in soap and let the water run hard. I picked up my guitar and a sense of weightlessness radiated throughout my body as I sat naked on the side of the bed with my testicles dangling free. A few minutes passed and Painin was out of the bathroom, putting her clothes on.

'Okay, you give money now. Two thousand baht.'

'What are you talking about? Where are you going?'

'I go work. You want see me again, you give money!'

'What?'

'Yes. You give money—NOW!'

'Look, Painin,' I said, knowing she wasn't playing around, 'I came to Laos because I wanted to be with you as your boyfriend, not your customer! I already told you I'll try and help with money, but this is crazy! Why are you doing this? I love you.'

'You think I like man? I not like any man. Many men want me, but I not care! You give two thousand baht or I break this,' she said, picking up my guitar tuner and looking at me with sharpened eyes.

'I can't! It's not right.'

Painin gave me one last look of disgust and threw my guitar tuner against the floor. It skidded towards the door and smashed against the wall.

'You not give money, I tell police! I tell my friend come fight you.'

Tears began to well up as her face flushed. I held her eyes and pleaded with her to calm down.

'Please, Painin,' I whimpered. 'I love you. I want to build a family with you. I want to help, but it can't be like this ...'

'Don't say anything.'

She got to her feet and walked out, leaving the door open. My head spun, my heart danced. I sat on the corner of the bed with my head between my hands and stared across the room.

Dumped ... first time in seven years.

A strange constrictive pain tore away at my ribs. Tears splashed between my toes, soaking slow into the dirty wooden floor. I kept staring out the window. *That's it ... the last time I'll ever see her. FUCK! How could she dump me?*

I decided to get arseholed, pulled out my bag of aunty and fired it up on a freshly punctured can bong. Gorgeous grey smoke raced down my gullet and sat inside my lungs. When I was good and ready, I pushed it out against the closed window and watched it cloud over my pathetic reflection.

The guy behind the reception desk was happy to let me change to another room. I threw my bag inside and walked into the street.

Brenton Rossow is the lead singer of The Folding Chairs. His work has been published in *Thieves Jargon, Parameter Magazine, Barrel House, Dogzplot, Decomp Mag, Jerseyworks, Flutter, Zygote in My Coffee, Nefarious Ballerina, Unlikely 2.0, Cha, The New Writer, Weyfarers, Qwerty* and *Indigo Journal* among others.

The Service Provider

John Burdett

Penny would never have described herself as a lady of the night, and, since she was white, British, and never walked the streets, neither would anyone else. In her heart, though, she admitted that for quite some time she had lived off men who would not have paid her expenses if she had not rendered a reasonable performance in bed.

She felt no guilt or degradation, only a mild anger. Not toward men. If anything, it was feminism she blamed for her situation. She adhered to the outdated female archetype who, in past times, settled down with a big-hearted man who forgave incompetence in housekeeping, cooking and the acquisition of money in return for an infinite tolerance combined with an unlimited affection for him and their children. In her dreams, she saw herself in a big untidy house with a big untidy garden (probably Bloomsbury between the wars: she had a fondness for history), a husband with a comfortable beer gut and scruffy kids who chased each other around the house and loved her. But in the twenty-first century, the chances of meeting any guy with a decent income who was not stressed out of his brain were as remote as winning the lottery.

So, in the way of the English today, she lived for vacations.

Through hints and prods, she had induced all of her last five boyfriends to take her on holiday, three times to the Med and twice to Morocco. The ending never changed. She would give him a great time, and through subtle female techniques ensure that he relax, let go, share his heart. She would assure him she was not looking for a marriage that would enable her to grab half his assets. Once he was suitably mellow, she would even allow herself to start to love him. Then the vacation would finish, they would fly back to London and within twenty-four hours he was a stressed-out, insufferable maniac all over again.

The last one had differed only in that she had seen failure coming. It had been her first time in Greece and, despite the excessive tourism, the islands had seduced her like nowhere else. She told him she didn't want to go back. She just couldn't face London anymore. She was sorry. He seemed to understand. He even financed her for a couple of months and flew out for a weekend, which she made sure was as dirty as could be—pulled out all the stops, so to speak, rolled, licked, sucked and humped the nights away until she felt as if she'd worked out in a gym; but they both knew it was the end of the affair. Keeping a mistress on a Greek island was almost as financially ruinous as marriage itself

So she hung out first on Crete, then on Mykonos, then on Lesbos for a few months until money started to get really tight. She became almost blatant about her pickups, made it clear that although no way was she on the game she was rather short of the readies *if you know what I mean, love* ... And so made her way slowly west.

She knew that in Gibraltar there were Brits with dough who

worked there. It seemed ideal, and only twelve miles from Morocco, where she had had a great holiday with number ... Well, she'd stopped counting, but it had been a great vacation.

She was disappointed. The Brits on the Rock were of the yobbish, loutish sort, many of them army or ex-army. Only by chance she made a contact who got her invited to a party given by a man from South London who was a prince of offshore gambling. It was a big, loud party in a big loud mansion in Sotto Grande, which is where rich Gibraltarians invariably live.

The host had little conversation and less manners, but he introduced her to Mike. Mike had no conversation at all and probably no manners—it was hard to say, he was so intense about an Internet game he'd invented that was earning him millions, something to do with dropping virtual balls into virtual boxes. He probably figured he didn't need any social graces. If she hadn't been desperate, she would have slapped him, his come-on was so crude. But at the same time, she could see he was honest, as the emotionally retarded can be. He really did think that people were basically computers and would do what you wanted if you clicked on the right spot. He guessed—it wasn't difficult considering how worn her best jeans and T-shirt were—that in her case he only needed to click on *dough*.

From the party mansion, it was only a short walk to his mansion, but he drove her in his Porsche. She knew the first night was a test; if she performed right, he would be quite generous. So, feeling like a real whore for the first time in her life, she pulled out all the stops. Next morning, he offered her a contract and left her, open-mouthed, to think about it while he drove over to Gib to make another million.

Sitting in the great big kitchen of the great big mansion, she felt suicidal. Had she really come to this? Out of sarcasm she wrote down the deal he had offered her in his snappy, take-it-or-leave-it, barrow-boy voice before he'd dashed out of the house without even a peck on the cheek.

She was not of the self-destructive kind, though, and knew very well there was a price to pay for everything. Considering how she'd pretty much sold her body for peanuts up to now, it wasn't really such a bad deal. Once she accepted the no-frills attitude, she realized he was being quite generous. She had trained as a legal secretary, but had proved unable to endure the tedium. Now she translated his hurried, staccato offer into legalese:

Between
Penelope Smith ('the Service Provider') of the first part
and Michael James Hope ('the Client') of the second part,
it is hereby agreed as follows:

1. The Service Provider will satisfy on demand any request of a sexual nature made by the Client at anytime of the day or night on receipt of not less than fifteen minutes notice provided that:

> *a. such request shall not cause pain, injury or risk of health to the Service Provider. (In this context, bondage and/or mild flagellation which does not break the skin shall not be considered painful or injurious to health; but the Service Provider shall have the right to refuse anal intercourse at her discretion.)*

b. For the avoidance of doubt, it is specifically agreed that the Service Provider will participate in group sex at the Client's request, provided that said group sex shall not include other men or more than two other women per session.

2. In return for the services set out in 1 above ('the Services'), the Client shall:

a. Pay the Service Provider five hundred pounds per week;

b. Provide accommodation at the Client's mansion in Sotto Grande free of charge, including a bedroom for the Service Provider's exclusive use;

c. Pay all reasonable living expenses of the Service Provider, including appropriate clothing and food, and provide a car for the Service Provider's exclusive use.

d. Purchase health insurance for the Service Provider.

For the avoidance of doubt and protection against disease, the Service Provider shall not engage in sexual activity with any person, male or female, other than the Client for the duration of the contract. It is explicitly agreed that the Service Provider will not entertain any person at the Client's home address, male or female, will not make noise or in any way disturb the Client's peace and quiet which he requires for his work, will not complain in any way about the Client's behaviour, manners, living habits, snoring, masturbation, taste in music, drinking, use of recreational drugs, involvement with other women, or, generally, assume in any way, manner or form the rights or privileges of a wife.

3. Either party may terminate this Agreement by providing seven days notice to the other party.

Signed:

Penelope Smith (Service Provider)

Michael James Hope (Client)

When he dashed in again that night, he said, 'Still here then?'

She showed him what she had written, expecting a laugh, or a snigger, or at least some sign of humour. Instead he nodded, took out a pen and signed. When he gave her the pen, she signed as well.

2.

All went according to plan. She thought of him as an over-sexed robot, but was able to tolerate the arrangement mostly because he was out of the house for at least twelve hours a day, working the phones and the email from tax-exempt Gibraltar, and thinking up more stupid ideas for making money out of still more stupid people. At night, she stayed in her room watching DVDs and Sky TV. When he wanted her, he called her on the house intercom. When he was finished, she went back to her own bed.

She came to understand the reference to drugs in the contract. He used some kind of speed while he was at work, and in the evenings when he wanted to slow down he used some kind of muscle relaxant. And, of course, like all good geeks, he loved marijuana. On Friday nights, he would take something stronger: a morphine-based tranquilizer which made him almost catatonic. His penis was the only organ still functioning. He would lie on his back with a deeply smug look on his face and tell her what he wanted in a hoarse whisper.

Even the bondage and flagellation were not as humiliating as she'd expected. That was because she was a tad partial to both, so long as they were done right. She'd once had a boyfriend who was adept at making a girl horny. He had whispered in her ear, whilst working her clitoris, about how he was going to tie her up to a tree and rape her; make her meet him in a dark alley wearing only a raincoat and have her against a rough brick wall; put her on all fours and whip her while he plunged deep inside her. In the event, he had done none of these things, perhaps because the stories and the finger work made her come in less than five minutes—but the seeds had been sown.

So when the Robot decided it was time to enforce that part of the contract, she wasn't too fearful. She was surprised he had the good taste to purchase thick velvet bonds with which he tied her hands and feet to the bed—she had been afraid thin nylon string would leave telltale marks. With all responsibility for everything taken from her shoulders, she found she could relax while he plunged away. Not for very long, though, the process raised such a stalk on him, he was finished in minutes.

The flagellation was the same, only more so. It seemed to her she had hardly roused herself to get on all fours and receive a half dozen tentative slaps with the whip—not more than harsh caresses really—when he expired in a heap and called for his dope. It was, of course, the state of dominance he craved. He was a control freak but not a violent man at all.

She did not know any other prostitutes, so could not compare experiences. She admitted that in terms of the retail of flesh, her situation was more Harrods than Tesco, but speaking only for herself, she had never had an easier job. Most of the time he was able to stimulate her enough for intercourse. When she was dry and not in the mood, she applied KY Jelly immediately after the fifteen-minute warning. He never lasted a full hour no matter what the variations.

She really didn't know what all the fuss was about. Surely women had been doing this one way or another for the hundred thousand years humans had been on earth? She could imagine herself in a previous incarnation as a cavewoman giving head in return for boiled mammoth knuckle. It was money for old rope— and best of all, she didn't have to cook or clean the house. He always ate takeaway from the box, and a Spanish maid, whom Penny supervised in an indulgent way, came three times a week. In return, the maid accorded her the full respect due to a rich man's pampered mistress.

The months passed, she spent not a penny of her salary and enjoyed passing time on the beach during the day reading romantic historical novels to which she was addicted. Quite a few men showed an interest in her when she lay in her bikini on a towel—she was under thirty, pretty with a voluptuous body and owned that magic something which said '*good in bed*'—but she brushed them off, not only to keep faith with the contract, but because most of the time she was sexually exhausted. He may have been a sprinter more than a long distance runner, but the Robot was perpetually aroused by having a non-nagging sex slave at his command, and— looking at it from a slightly deeper point of view—obviously had no idea what to do with his fellow human beings other than to fuck them, whether virtually in Gib or literally in Sotto Grande. Only one thing intrigued her. He had made group sex a specific requirement, but so far there had been no sign of it. She was soon to realize why.

3.

'We're going to Bangkok,' he snapped.

'When?'

'Day after tomorrow. Got two first-class ticks from Rabat via Dubai—better than bloody London. We'll get whatever's going from here to Rabat. Ferry, then a limo, prob'ly. Start tomorrow.' He looked at her. 'See, I don't have the energy for threesomes while I'm working. This is vac time. Don't worry, I only go for pretty ones. Might want a few holiday pix though.'

'I'll start packing.'

'Carry-on only, I don't want to hang around waiting for check-in luggage. I'll buy whatever when we arrive. Silk's cheap over there. Might buy some for bondage.' He rubbed his hands.

The Robot had been to Thailand before and knew where to go. He took her to Patpong where they watched young brown women remove ping-pong balls and razor blades from their private parts, but this was only the warm-up. Later they went to a place called Nana where near-naked girls strutted their stuff on stage and a man could take his pick.

On the plane, he had told her what he meant by group sex. It would be her job to explain it to the girl once they got back to the hotel. To her surprise, he wanted to discuss with her which girl to choose. She found they had opposite tastes. He tended to go for the slightly taller, more assertive types while she liked the cute, petite ones.

At the end of the day though, for him it came down to tits. He hired one with large, firm mammaries and they took her back in the taxi like a pet. It was strange the way they both went out of their way to be nice to her—kindness itself, actually. She spoke almost no English, though, so Penny had to use sign language to explain:

Phase I:	blowjob for Boss by guest worker while staff member gets licked by Boss;
Phase II:	guest worker licks staffer while staffer gives head;
Phase III:	Boss takes pix of guest worker lubricating staffer with her tongue;
Phase IV:	guest worker gets under staffer to lick Boss while Boss rogers staffer.

When it was over, Mike slept between them and for the first time seemed to be at peace.

They repeated the exercise a couple of times with different girls, then Mike decided he wanted to spend a few days in the country. He'd done the beach thing too many times before; he wanted the mountains. Of course, if it was going to be for more than one night, it would have to be the right girl. On instinct, they chose one who was slightly older, perhaps late twenties. Her name was Om and she was from the mountains herself, so she would be a good guide. The Robot bought first-class tickets for all of them and off they flew to Mai Hong Song.

He found a hotel with large rooms and immediately demanded an orgy. Penny and Om already knew what to do from the night before, but this time everything had slowed down, perhaps because of the journey, the heat and the proximity of the jungle.

She didn't know why she thought the jungle made a difference, it just came into her head. When the moment came for her to lay on her back with his hard-on in her mouth and Om gently, patiently working her vagina with her tongue, she too felt an extraordinary serenity, a sense of relief of flesh surrounded by friendly flesh. Afterwards, Om grinned at her for coming so quickly.

By the next night, Penny had realized there was something very special about Om. The young Thai woman remained friendly and unfazed by anything they did together. She treated Penny as a pal and would tug at her breasts in a chummy way, as if they were sisters. She liked it when Penny did the same back. Om even gave Mike's cock friendly, non-erotic tugs from time to time, always with the same serenity, never losing her dignity.

This had a strange effect on Mike. He became even quieter than normal, watched Om with an increasingly gaping mouth, as if she were some kind of superior alien being.

It wasn't supposed to last long. Mike had planned for a ten-day vacation and had booked the return trip, but just when they were due to leave Mae Hong Song, he contracted some kind of stomach infection that left him pretty much nailed to the bed. He postponed the flight home.

He was fine in a couple of days, but strangely reluctant to leave. He asked Om where her home village was. She told him it was on the border with Burma, just a few miles away. He asked if they could go there. She said they could, but she could not have sex with them there—it would be strictly a case of her acting as guide. Penny was surprised that Mike agreed to this.

Om's village was really a collection of smallholdings where her kinsfolk grew rice and—secretly, up in the hills—opium. So there was no problem finding opium for Mike. Now he was really relaxed. The only problem: he wanted to sleep between Om and Penny. Om said that was okay, they would be like family—so long as there was no sex. How would anyone know if they were having sex or not, the three of them? Om seemed surprised at the question. She said it was obvious if three people were having sex together or not.

'But you've both gotta be naked, right?' Mike said.

Om said that would be okay; it was so damn hot, she only wore a sarong anyway.

So they ended up in a bamboo hut with a springy bamboo floor, on the edge of dense jungle, with Mike smoking his opium and gratefully—blissfully—lying between them like a baby, wallowing in the proximity of unlimited naked female flesh.

For the first time, he began to talk like a real human. How awful his home life was: an alcoholic father, hard bitch for a mother, brothers all in prison, mostly for burglary and armed robbery. A hell he'd only escaped thanks to his gift for computer science and Internet games. 'You think I'm weird? That lot can hardly talk at all,' he said.

When he was in an opium dream, Penny talked to Om. She told the guest worker about her contract with Mike.

'He's not so bad, really. Very screwed up, but actually honourable. I mean, he does everything he promised under the contract, he just can't seem to relate to people, that's all.'

Om said she didn't see anything different about him from other *farang*. Penny took this to include herself—did she strike Om as a female version of Mike?

'Of course,' Om said with a smile.

'You mean a total mess, don't you?'

'I mean very sick,' Om said.

She then explained that she had only gone on the game for a short while to pay off a debt her mother had incurred purchasing medicine for her father who had recently died. Thanks to Mike, she would be able to pay off the debt. When Mike and Penny had gone, she would become a *mai chee*: a Buddhist nun. She wanted to spend the rest of her life in meditation.

Now Penny thought she understood Om's dignity. As far as the Thai woman was concerned, she was not practicing a form of debauchery so much as administering therapy to two pink-faced psychotics.

When Penny thought about it, she tended to agree. She had

looked down on Mike as being sub-human—but was she really so different herself? It was the leap of imagination that was hard to make at first, until you got used to it: the West as the source of a world psychosis that was destroying humanity.

When you put it like that in so many words, it seemed obviously true. Look at how people were today: spoilt brats at best, enraged loonies in their hearts most of the time.

'We all hate each other,' she admitted to Om, with a gasp.

Om nodded and told Penny she should meditate. She explained that Mike had to have opium because he was too far gone to meditate, he would never break through the reinforced concrete of his ego, but for Penny, a woman with a good heart, there was a chance.

Now Penny found herself encouraging Mike with his opium habit, so she could stay on a few more days with Om and learn to meditate. Both women made sure Mike had plenty of *fin* to keep him quiet while they went to temple and sat in silence in a semi-lotus position. Penny knew she was slow in spiritual matters, but not entirely without talent. With Om's help, she developed a vague understanding of the ancient teaching and an appreciation of the peace it could bring to the heart.

When Mike was able to walk, which happened for a couple of hours in the evening of each day, he would wander into the jungle and sit on a fallen tree trunk. That must have been where he caught cerebral malaria.

Penny flew into a panic. She didn't want a person's death on her conscience; she wanted to get him to a hospital in the UK straight away, but Om wasn't so keen. She thought that if Mike died there in her village surrounded by monks whispering into his ear, there was a chance he would be reborn as a human, maybe even as a Thai Buddhist, so he would have a great chance of personal evolution in his next life.

If he went back to the West, on the other hand, even if he was in time to be cured, he would just go back to his old ways and be reborn as a rat or something even lower down the scale.

Penny gulped. This was another leap she was not prepared for. Her mind immediately thought up a good old British compromise: suppose they got him to Bangkok and, when he was better, introduce him to Buddhism? Okay, he might not achieve a human rebirth that way, but he could maybe reach monkey or chimpanzee level— further up the scale than rat, anyway. She hardly realized how her thinking had changed under Om's influence.

'I'll do whatever you want,' Om said with a smile.

Penny understood this was some kind of test the Buddha was putting her through. Had she got the message strongly enough to dare to do let Mike die?

Mercifully, for the Buddha was nothing if not compassionate, the decision was made for her. Mike succumbed to the particularly virulent form of the disease in just over thirty-six hours. Om made sure that nine monks sat around his deathbed connected by a piece of white string and chanting in a way that his spirit could hear and understand.

After they had burned his body in the temple oven, Penny said: 'I want to stay here, but I could never be a nun—I don't have your kind of strength.'

'I know,' Om said.

185

As it happened, one of her brothers had recently lost his wife, also to malaria. He was a good big-hearted guy, if a bit lazy, with a huge beer gut and a big sprawling house full of scruffy kids just down the road ...

John Burdett was brought up in North London and attended Warwick University where he read English and American Literature. This left him largely unemployable until he re-trained as a barrister and went to work in Hong Kong. He made enough money there to retire early to write novels. To date he has published six novels, including the Bangkok series: *Bangkok 8*, *Bangkok Tattoo*, *Bangkok Haunts* and *The Godfather of Kathmandu*.

SINGAPORE

Mirrors

Christopher Taylor

1. Caroline

He is reclining in his leather armchair, reading the newspaper and she is watching him from the other side of the room. She has just come home from work. She has mixed a gin and tonic, easy on the tonic. She sips the bitter liquid and watches him flip the page.

'What's new?' she says.

'The world is fucked,' he says.

'Lucky world,' she says. He doesn't react. She takes a few paces, stops behind the armchair and puts a hand on his shoulder. 'Anything I should care about?' she says.

'Another stewardess has been raped ... Forest fires in Sumatra. Protests outside terrorist trial in Manila.'

'Nothing new, then.' Her hand slides up his collarbone, her thumb massaging the back of his neck.

'How was work?' he says.

'Oh, you know. I'm still working on that deal, the one with Jakarta. Lim's still his pig-headed, sexist self. Company stocks holding up surprisingly well, considering.'

His gaze flicks back and forth. She sits on the arm of his chair and lets her hand rest casually on his chest. He manoeuvres his arm around hers to turn another page of the newspaper. She looks out of the plate glass windows beyond the balcony to the golf course, and further, to Sentosa Island and the harbour. 'Manchester won,' he says.

Some time passes, and then she says, 'How about Bintan?'

'For what?'

'For a weekend.'

'Ya, okay. Can.'

'Okay. I'll book it.'

'Wait. What weekend? I have golf next three ones.'

'Honey,' she says, looking her husband straight in the eye. He looks up at her, meets her gaze and smiles. 'Can you make an excuse? Let's just go. Can't we?' He frowns. This is not part of his plan, she can see that. For a moment, she is intensely annoyed with him, almost to the point of hatred. But then she thinks, *Of course: everyone is like this. Nobody really wants to be spontaneous.* And she doesn't really want to go to Bintan anyway; it's a stupid island, covered in golf courses.

'Can ...' he says, half-heartedly, but she knows he is saying it to please her. It would be better if he just refused. She walks to the window and looks out. She hears the rustle of paper behind her. She turns and looks at him, then, with a purpose, walks back to the chair and kneels down.

'Keep reading your paper,' she says as she unzips his trousers and slides her slim fingers with their fuschia-polished nails inside. 'Keep reading, honey.'

2. Lim

'The amazing thing is, when you perfect this ...I can't call it a technique, lah. It's more like a kind of ... attitude. The thing is, what I'm getting at, they come to you. You don't even have to try. I mean this girl ... married. And beautiful. Seriously.

'I mean, she was just there for eye candy, right? That's why we employ these MBA babes, to flick their rebonded hair and flutter the lashes. Clicky clicky on the mouse, oh-so-deh-lick-cate-ly. I could see these Jakarta guys getting all hot under the collar when she went through her Powerpoint slides. I want her to say, "Oops, I dropped my pencil, lah" and just, you know, bend over in that tight skirt, but she doesn't have to. The professionality of this girl is much more of a turn-on, and when she walked up and fingered that laser pointer, I knew we had them. I was hard already from the fucking, excuse my French, from the deal. I just had to reel them in like fish. Too easy.

'So, anyway, the point is, I had no designs, absolutely none on this girl. I mean, she's married, I even played golf with her hubby once. I was quite shagged out anyway, you know what I mean, I went straight from Geylang to the airport and into the damn meeting and there I was, wired on coffee and just kind of winging it. We were in the hotel bar afterwards, and I was just thinking about my big, fat bonus, and it turns out she was thinking about my big fat boner ... Sorry, lah, sorry. I know, I know, don't cover your ears, it's okay, I just get carried away telling the story. So damned sweet.

'Anyway, there we are, in the hotel bar, at the bar, drinking Chivas and green tea to celebrate. I've got one eye on her, one on the television, which is showing the news, nothing interesting, no football, just some kind of riot being put down in the Philippines.

And she says "So how is Mrs Lim?" and I'm like "She's a wonderful woman, I would do anything for her, she's a saint" because I'm in such a good mood. And is she pouting just a little at this? I don't know, they always look like they're pouting a little bit anyway, and anyway I don't notice, and she says "Your wife really understands you, then?". And I say "Well I suppose she does, as much as anyone understands anyone else" because I'm kind of a philosopher sometimes, you know me.

'Anyway, then she says something like "I have a wonderful marriage, my husband is taking me to Bintan next weekend" and I say that's nice, and I drink some more Chivas, and she gives me a really long, kind of weird look, like I've said something really irritating, and after while, she says "How about Champagne?". And I say "I think that is a very wonderful idea, and the company would be delighted to pay for us to drink Champagne given how we have nailed the Jakartans and all", and so she orders a bottle and we polish it off in about twenty minutes, and by this point I suddenly start to think perhaps she might be MBA in more ways than one ...

'What? You never heard that one? Married But Available ... ha ha ... anyway, at this point I am definitely starting to suspect that something may be on the cards, so I'm thinking, well I will just try something subtle, so I say "Have you checked the movies on the hotel TV?" and she says "Let's go check them now" and she orders another bottle of Champagne and off we are going upstairs, leaning on each other and the walls but we get to her room, and ...

'No, lah. No, I know you don't want to know the saucy details, man, but seriously, her ass is the cutest thing I ever saw. Oh my god. Sorry, lah. Sorry. You're such a good guy. I think it's just my hormonal make-up or something. I am overactive in that department ever since I was—hey, beer, over here!—well, you know me.

'Well, if you insist. Yes, we did. Yes, she was. I mean, seriously, I never … the things she can do with those hands, even though I was a bit drunk and all. And I hardly had to move a muscle, just lay back and let it all happen. There was a movie on the TV too. It was a funny one, you know, that American one, with the students. Pie something.'

3. Marlene

She cannot decide whether he is an Epic or a Romantic. Clearly, according to the theory, he must be one or the other. So, she must work it out: which one is he?

It was not clear at first even that he was one of those two. It has taken her some time to narrow it down. But now he is inside her, pushing into her over and again, and she is lying there on her belly, her face muffled in the pillow while he shunts behind her and she tries to work it out.

Consider the evidence, she thinks. For the Epic hypothesis: he cheats. Clearly. Repeatedly. This is obvious. And he doesn't feel guilty. The Romantics still do it, but they have this tragic look on their faces, like they hate themselves. He doesn't have that.

On the other hand, he clearly knows what he wants. There is a routine to this for him, she can see it. There is not enough adventure in this for him for it to be an Epic encounter.

So, it's an enigma. Unless, that is, there might be a new category. What would she call it? She frowns.

He finishes with a grunt and rolls over. She waits the usual length of time before showering, puts her clothes back on, checks herself in the mirror, and kisses him on the cheek.

'Thanks,' he says.

'Welcome,' she says, and heads out to the street, getting into a taxi. When the driver drops her off at the shopping centre, she picks her way up a halted escalator to the second floor, and shows her ID at the entrance to Club Island.

Inside, the band has started. A group of Western guys is being served beer. She stands nearby. One of them is very drunk, wearing a fright wig, a dog collar and a pair of frilly pink panties over the top of his jeans. 'My fiance,' he is saying, 'is the best ... the best ... you know. Lovely, lovely, lovely. Lovely Keiko. I bloody love her.'

Marlene walks into his line of sight and gives him the look. He glances at her and smiles. *Mine,* she thinks.

As she is walking over to the group, it comes to her. *That Chinese businessman does need a new category*, she thinks, and now she knows what it is.

4. Keiko

Seven weeks of silence
I break on you like a wave
Why are you absent?

Follow in bare feet
We trace our cold apartment
Our soles on cool tiles

You, the setting sun
Falling always away from me
I run too slowly

Dark air between us
My fingers ask a question
Half your heart answers

Divide and divide
Love leaks, an ebbing fluid
Diminishing us

When did you leave me?
Why did I not notice it?
I don't understand

5. Brett

No work this week. Only essential travel to the Philippines is advised. Unrest has spread from the cities to the countryside. The rice fields are alight. Some flights are cancelled, including the ones he was due to pilot.

He arrives at Boat Quay at seven-fifteen and takes a table by the river, ordering a Heineken. Jazz drifts from the bar next door. Luminous towers dwarf the shophouses.

She arrives. He checks her out—small, cute—he approves—before standing and waving to catch her attention. She has the slightly knock-kneed gait of many Japanese women, as if modestly keeping her legs together. He will see about that.

He has made the most of these free evenings, and this is his fourth date of the week. God bless date-or-not.com, he thinks.

'So, you're an airline pilot,' she says. 'That must be very interesting.'

It's a good sign. Impressed by his job. He checks her out subtly while sipping his beer. She will certainly do.

He is already thinking about the mirrors on his ceiling, how she will look, how he will look doing it to her when he sees them reflected. He has lost weight recently, buffed up a bit. He spent a full twenty-five minutes before heading out examining his reflection in the full-length wall mirror in his bedroom.

'You have lovely ears,' he says. He means it. She really does. Each woman has her own special part of the body, he thinks. Like Juvita, the air hostess who kept blowing him in the aircraft toilets. Perfect neck. Tragic what happened to her.

'Thank you,' Keiko says, modestly. She insists on pouring his beer for him.

'Would you like to see a great view of the city?' he says.

'Of course,' she says.

She is under him, her eyes wide. He shifts position so that she is on top. He grasps her slim hips with both hands, then lets the back of one graze across the gentle curve of her breasts, feeling the hard small nipples against his skin. Her mouth is open in a silent exclamation, her eyes tight shut, pelvis rocking. He glances upwards, taking in the sight of her moving on him, and his own body, taught under her. She opens her eyes, looks upwards, then squeezes them tightly shut again and digs her nails into his chest. For a moment, he looks up into his own eyes as if into those of an adversary, one who acknowledges him silently in the dimly lit room.

6. Juvita

She meets Andrew at her tennis club. They have sex that afternoon, in the showers of the ladies' changing rooms, with the water running. They have sex at dusk, behind a bush in the Botanical Gardens, and in his car, and in the disabled toilets at the Esplanade in the interval of a classical concert, and on the beach on Bintan, and in every room of his apartment, and she sucks him off in the cable car between Harbour Front and Sentosa and wanks him off in the back of a multiplex on Orchard Road during a car chase. He is her thirty-second lover since it happened.

'I love you,' he says one day. She stops returning his calls.

7. Andrew

May is cooking rice and some kind of Japanese soup with seaweed in it. He stands in the kitchen with her, opens the wine and pours it into two blue-tinged, thick-stemmed glasses. *The trick is not to look too desperate*, he thinks. He discreetly checks out her buttocks and then feels guilty.

'How was your friend's birthday?' he says.

'Not bad,' she says, tasting the soup. 'Although we had a few too many, I'm afraid.' He chuckles complicitly. 'We had to send the birthday girl home early in a taxi. And then I got talking to a very nice couple, and, um, did that for a while. And then Saturday was shopping. How about you?' She stirs more rapidly.

199

'Pretty boring, I'm afraid,' he says. 'I just watched the news. Seems the Philippine thing has spread.'

'Really?' she says, absently. The rice cooker light flicks from red to amber.

'I hope I'm getting some sex tonight,' she says as he takes the last spoonful of soup. He swallows heavily and looks at her, startled. 'It doesn't have to be right now,' she adds quickly. 'We can let our food settle first. Drink?'

Several very large gin-and-tonics later, he gets up, sits down, gets up again and they stagger together to her room. He fiddles with the portable CD player while she removes her clothes and lies back, ready. Barry White starts playing. They laugh together at the cheesiness of his choice. He falls back next to her and begins kissing her. Her tongue probes his mouth. He clutches her breasts, then licks them. She makes noises of approval.

He pushes his hand down inside her panties and fingers her. She is already wet. He finds her clitoris and makes small circles with his finger. He pulls off her, and then his own, underwear. She lies back, legs open, eyes closed.

After a little while, his member is still, at most, half-mast. The room is turning gin-flavoured circles around his head, which he lowers to the bed to rest a little. It is a little worrying, but he optimistically reasons that if he just carries on, eventually things will sort themselves out.

He is about to suggest that she offer him a hand when she speaks. 'Can I say something direct?' she says. His middle digit keeps making small circles, the room large ones. 'If all I wanted was a finger,' she says, 'I wouldn't have bothered to cook for someone. I could have done that on my own.'

'Sorry,' he says.

'Perhaps,' she says,' you would like to just talk some more. We could exchange knitting patterns. Would you like to do that instead?'

He withdraws his hands from her and lies staring at the curtains. She sighs and looks him in the eyes.

'Let me introduce you to my best friend,' she says. She reaches under the bed and pulls out a smooth black dildo, a foot and a half long. His eyes widen. She grasps it two-handed, rolls sideways and impales herself on it, groaning convulsively as she comes, and then lies still, smiling. It is like watching someone commit Japanese ritual suicide.

Andrew gets up and pulls on his boxer shorts. 'I have to go,' he says.

'Really?' she says, looking surprised. 'Why?'

8. May

'That just gave me a great idea for a story.'

'You want me to stop?'

'No ... just. Ah. No ... Listen. I'm thinking ...'

'Seriously, Alex, at least finish fucking me before you start work.'

'Okay ...'

'Okay ... Ah. Yes.'

'...'

'Is that good, baby?'

'It's … um. Yes.'

'Yes?'

'Yes … in the conflict. It's set on one of the rebel-held islands …'

'Oh, for God's sake. I'm not going to stop, you know.'

'No … keep going, it's good.'

'I know. I'm damn good. They all say that.'

'…'

'Oh …'

'… and the rebel leader has a kind of harem, of girls from the local population …'

'For fuck's sake, Alex.'

'Sorry … Ah! Is that a new trick?'

'Do you like it?'

'… but his favourite one escapes, and it kind of ruins his … Oh My Fucking Christ … Ah!'

'Okay, I give up. Keep going with the story. I'll just …'

'Jesus. And he goes looking for the girl …'

'Wait, let me try it like this.'

'And he finds her. In a …'

'In a?'

'In a brothel, in a local town …'

'…'

'… and he can't touch her any more, because to him it's as if she was … polluted.'

'People are shit.'

'Yep. This guy especially so.'

'…'

'Oh.'

'Touch me here.'

'... and he's so pissed off that he goes back to the jungle and brings his rebels and burns down the brothel and burns and massacres half the town for good measure, just out of pique ...'

'...'

'... and after the battle, he's in his tent and a girl comes in at night and ...'

'And ...?'

'... and does ... what you just did ... and it ... blows his ...'

'Uhuh?'

'... ah ... his mind. And he wakes up next morning and sees that it's the same girl, escaped from the burning brothel.'

'And?'

'... and he realizes the error of his ways and embraces true love.'

'...'

'Oh God, May ...'

'Okay ...'

'Don't stop ... keep going ...'

'That's it. That's it. Oh yes. Yes. Yes. Yes.'

'Jesus ... fucking ... Christ ... on a ... fucking ... bike ...'

'...'

'...'

'That was good.'

'You're not kidding.'

'But you know what?'

'What?'

'Your story sucks.'

9. Alex

You have to be fucking kidding me. A *dude*?

10. Nong

She tucks her dick and balls between her legs and slips on the tight black trousers. Arranges her silicon tits inside purple lace. Practices her pout in the mirror. She is picked up and driven to the ambassador's residence, showing her ID at the manned gate. 'Hello Baby,' she says to him.

They spend the evening doing all the things he likes, which are many and varied, and include, after the semen has dried on the sheets and used condoms litter the floor, talking about the international situation.

Over these last months, she has offered her advice on various matters, but this is the most important. Now the trouble has spread to several countries, including her own, and his country is considering sending in its military in support of its allies. Tomorrow's negotiation is, as he puts it, the crunch. She worries for him. She soothes him, says kind things, thoughtful things, insightful things. He will consider her advice, he says. Then she leaves, discreetly picking up the envelope of cash from the table on her way out to where a limousine is waiting, the driver trying not to make it obvious that he is staring from the side of his eyes in a fascination he would not admit to in front of his friends.

11. Charles

She asked him for a favour. There were so few flights, and her family were all back there, her children also, and she missed them, she was worried, and she was very sorry to ask and to bother him but she was due the vacation and he was so important and so smart, could he get her back home for Christmas? No, he said, too dangerous, the jungle is full of terrorists, but when she wept, he couldn't stand it. He relented and pulled a string or two. She was booked on one of the few flights still operating to Cebu City.

Now, in the quiet of the early evening, with the dark palms whispering outside in the garden and deep-throated bullfrogs honking in the trees like a broken accordion, the ambassador returns to his house with a heavy heart. He sits in the leather armchair and rests his forehead in his hands. She brings him a glass of Highland Park with a single ice cube, and puts down a bowl of pistachio nuts.

He looks up at her. She has a kind face. 'Thank you, Rosa,' he says.

'Is there anything else I can do, Sir?' she asks. He says that there is not. She steps forward, takes his hand and touches it to her forehead.

What follows could be construed as exploitation, as abuse of his power over her. This thought certainly crosses his mind briefly during the act, but he dismisses it. When he comes, it is with a strange feeling of peace, as if all his striving, all his work is doomed to futility, but that he doesn't mind at all.

12. Rosa

Rosa is awake in the night. A gecko says "*geck*-oh" with the voice of a dog's squeaky bone. Insects chorus and then cease in unison at the sound of a shot in the forest. The air is close, unstirred.

The moon has disappeared now, and through the uncurtained

window, Rosa can see the silhouette of the volcano against a backdrop of stars. She wonders what the stars are. Are they angels in Heaven? Are they the souls of dead children? Are they the frozen tears of God?

She flies up to touch them.

She must have drifted into sleep because she did not notice him come in, but now a dark figure stands by her bed. She catches her breath, thinking that it is her husband, Reynante, come back from his hiding place in the forest. It is too dangerous, she thinks. If they catch him ... but this, after all, is why she has come back.

She cannot bear to open her eyes fully, so she pretends to be asleep and watches through quivering lashes. Something metallic is lowered gently to the floor. He stands, not moving, but he is looking at her, she can tell. *Go away*, she thinks. *Hide.*

Stay, she thinks.

She is sure he can hear her thoughts.

His breathing can now be heard, with the merest edge of a wheeze. She tries to remember how her husband breathes. Is it like this?

He lies down on the bed next to her. After some more time, a rough knuckle barely touches the skin of her belly, withdraws, then comes back, stroking her skin below the T-shirt. Her heart beats fast.

She closes her eyes and lets the tip of one small finger stray to where he is.

In the darkness, with the sound of the ocean and the forest outside, he enters her. And as he enters her, her soul leaves her body and flies up, away from this small house, up to the million stars; and she looks down on their two bodies making love, on the wooden house with the vegetables growing outside and the fishing boat hauled up on the black-sand beach, on the forest stretching up the side of the smoking mountain and on the islands all around, the thousands of sand-fringed islands in this calm sea, dotted by human souls. And as she feels him enter her again and again and clutches at him, she feels her soul rise higher, so that she can see the whole world, and every dwelling place in the world, and every couple who at that moment is making love; and for a moment, each couple is a fire, burning in the night, a flickering pinpoint of light on the curving dark map of the Earth.

And the sky above is a great mirror, stretching away to eternity all around, the fires reflected in its depths.

And suddenly she knows what the stars are.

Christopher Taylor was born in the north of England and has lived and worked in England, Zimbabwe and Singapore. He currently lives in Manchester, where he works as a mathematician.

Breaking Glass

Dawn Farnham

Slut, she thought as Alex ran his hand through his silky black hair. It was a movement which allowed his coat to fall open revealing the outline of his narrow waist and toned torso against his shirt. Within a second, his hair had fallen again, boyishly, onto his forehead.

She was looking at him over the rim of the coffee cup from inside her office. He was talking to one of the secretaries. *Talking to? Chatting up, sexing up more like*, she thought. He was a typical male slut. He was the director and star of his own show, moving the rest of the cast, women and men alike, like puppets. He used his looks and intelligence like a plunging neckline, to get what he wanted; success, status, approval, attention. But he was very, very good. It was effortless.

Apart from this one movement of his hand, he stood still when he talked to the girls in the office, a certain stillness that seemed to speak of depths, of virile assurance. We would go slow, it said, I'm a man with a slow hand. It was the girls that moved, swaying into him, inclining their empty heads towards his lips, putting out their hands to his arm as if was a magnet and they were iron filings.

Iron filings; it was good, she thought. Dancing around him like mindless shavings, throwing themselves against him, flattened, will-less, until he turned off the charm and they fell sliding to the floor.

He glanced towards her office. It was the tiniest movement of his eyes, but she saw it. She had studied him. At length. He was Chinese, like her, but he had come from privilege and old money, and she from the HDB Heartlands of Singapore. They were matched in education, credentials and abilities, but they'd got to this place along very different roads. Alex was the only thing that stood in her way to the top of one of the most powerful companies in the Lion City.

The week's events would decide which of them got the job of managing director in the company. The chairman was looking at retirement in a few years. Whoever got the job would be the next big boss. Level playing field, the chairman had said. He was a man of principle, of an old-fashioned kind of morality in life and in business, and she believed him. The glass ceiling was only cracked and splintered in many companies, but in this one, she felt she could smash it with her fist and reach the stars beyond. It was an incredible feeling.

Alex had tried very hard to charm her and she had been very careful to be casually and smilingly uncharmed. He was discreet, but women talked and she was certain of his intentions. The only way to get what he wanted was to discredit her. The only way he could do that was to seduce her.

He was tempting though, she had to admit, from the safety of her office as he walked down the corridor. He moved like a boxer, light on his feet, broad-shouldered, powerful, lithe, athletic. He was all promise. A promise of smouldering heat, skin on skin, of dreamy and intoxicating bliss. He stirred fantasies in a woman's head. Dangerous fantasies. She put down her coffee and took a long drink of cold water.

The four-day meeting with the clients was at an island resort. One of those places with seven-hundred-dollar-a-night native cabanas on a perfect tropical beach.

The island was erotically charged. It was ridiculous to bring a delegation of business executives and clients to such a place, away from husbands and boyfriends, wives and girlfriends. When she was boss, she'd make sure they had four-day conferences in tents in Siberia. Survival was just the thing to knock sex on the head.

Dinner was a pleasant affair, the clients happy, the food good, the wine flowing. Alex had offered a dance, but she had refused. Getting into proximity with him was not a good idea. As she left for her cabana, she saw he had his arms round one of the secretaries and felt a momentary twinge of envy, which quickly vanished.

She took a bath and changed into her nightgown, let down her long, glossy, black hair and looked at herself in the mirror. Thirty-nine, figure good, button nose, great eyes, skin still fresh, pert tits. She laughed and poured a glass of champagne.

There was a knock. Room service with more champagne, she hoped. Perhaps Siberia was a bit harsh.

'Suchen, sorry it's so late.'

Alex was standing at the door. His eyes left hers and dropped slowly down her body. It was a look of pure admiration. She had nothing on underneath this thin garment and, she suddenly realized, her breasts were outlined against the satin.

'Alex,' she said, unmoving. Let him look. See what he's missing for the rest of his life.

'Just need to see if we agree on some figures before tomorrow's big meeting. Whatever's happening between us, we can't look like fools in front of the clients.'

She looked down and saw his laptop. This was highly dubious and really not worthy of him.

'Tomorrow morning, early. At breakfast, plenty of time. Goodnight.'

The problem was her voice was steady, but her heart rate had risen. Damn the man, attractive bastard. She always avoided being close to him and now he was standing one foot away and with that infuriating magnetic stillness.

'Don't be iron filings, Suchen,' she said to herself. She took a breath and made to close the door. He put out his hand and she looked at him, indignant.

'What— ' she began.

'Sorry, orders from chairman. Check your phone.'

She frowned and turned. Her phone was on the bedside table and she looked at it. There was a message. It must have come in whilst she was in the bath. Some problem with the figures, he said. Check it out tonight.

When she turned back, Alex had closed the door, put his laptop on the desk and was looking at her. She suddenly realized she was in silhouette against the lamp and moved away.

He took off his coat and hung it on the back of the chair. He was wearing a white fitted T-shirt and it showed every dip and line of his flat abdomen and the muscles of his tanned arms.

Her mind began to spiral off in unwanted carnal directions. She felt an involuntary spasm between her legs.

Oh, no, no, she thought. *No, you don't.* 'Be right back.'

She grabbed some clothes and went into the bathroom. She tied her hair up in a thick elastic ribbon. When her hair was down, silky smooth to her waist, she felt wanton. That would not do at all. She could certainly not sit around working with no clothes on. Sensible cotton bra and panties, plain T-shirt and good solid jeans. These were proof against any man's charms. She looked at the bottle of champagne in the ice bucket.

A few minutes later she came out. 'Champagne?' she said, putting the ice bucket on the coffee table. Alex poured himself a glass and drank.

'Might be a long, hard night,' he said, refilling his glass. She raised an eyebrow. She was pretty sure he'd emphasized 'long' and 'hard'. Subtle, she thought. He smiled and finished the glass of champagne.

She opened her laptop and sat at the desk. Alex drew a chair next to hers. They worked on the figures and quickly saw the problem. In no time, they'd straightened it out. He was smart and quick and really a pleasure to work with.

His arm brushed hers.

Her mind began a downward spiral of swirling coloured lights, like the credits of a bad Seventies movie.

Alex's hand moved behind her. In a swift movement, he pulled the ribbon which bound her hair and it cascaded down her back.

'Suchen,' he whispered. 'You are really beautiful.'

She felt the rising beat of her blood. It was the hair making her wanton, and she searched for the ribbon.

'What do you think you're doing,' she said, and her breath was a gasp.

'Making love to you,' he said as he ran his fingers into her hair and held her head and his mouth was suddenly on her neck, his lips soft, soft, kissing her, small kisses up her neck, under her ear. She felt as if she was melting. When he moved his lips to her cheek and began kissing and nibbling her mouth, she found the willpower to pull away.

'Stop this, Alex,' she said thickly.

But he didn't stop, though she tried weakly to push him away. He took her hand and put it down between his legs. She felt the bulge and she could imagine the very cells of his blood coursing, expanding, engorging.

He took her mouth in his as if it was his right, a kiss of deep softness, and moved her hand on him, growing harder by the second.

'Do you want me to stop?' he murmured against her mouth.

Futile, was about the last thing she thought. 'No,' she breathed. 'Get naked.'

He stood, taking her with him. She sank to her knees in front of him as if she was at the altar of some erotic god. He took off his belt, slowly, like a damn striptease artist.

She licked her lips, waiting, like a child waits for candy. His pants dropped over his hips to the floor. He had no underwear and her eyes flew open and she took him into her mouth, moving her tongue and lips around and along him, listening to the cues of his moans. She wanted to taste every inch of this hard wonderful thing he owned, the feeling so strong, she began to kiss and lick him in a groaning frenzy.

Then he pulled away gently and leant down and brought her up to him. 'Too fast,' he said breathlessly. 'Wait.'

He took off her T-shirt. She scrambled to get out of her jeans, and by the time he'd taken off her bra, they were both naked. She went to the bed. *No subtlety here*, she thought dimly. He was hard and beautiful. She felt dripping with wetness, ready for him.

Not yet, the look in his bottomless brown eyes seemed to say. His hair fell over his face as he dropped his mouth to her breasts, leaning over her, the smooth skin of his chest touching her belly, his soft lips on her nipples, moving his tongue until she felt like fire. She clutched him, willing him to come into her, so ready she thought she might ignite. The thought made her smile, even in the midst of these swirling emotions.

'Alex,' she said.

'Not yet.'

He moved down her body, running his fingers into her wetness, then buried his head between her legs. She was not ready for the jolt which shook her as his tongue played with her, and she clutched his hair; *don't stop, don't stop*. The orgasm shook her, wave on wave sending her body into delicious, mind-darkening spasms.

As the light returned dimly, he rose and pushed himself inside her, sliding silky, thickly smooth and her hips rose to him, her body shuddering with absolute, mind-altering desire. She wound her arms around his perfect neck and slipped down the path of ecstasy.

They moved like great dancers, each movement a whispered response the one to the other, until she felt a rush of blood so powerful it pounded in her ears and she clutched him to her, wanting to enter his body, melt into his flesh. The orgasm lifted her hips off the bed and a river of hot liquid ran over him, drenching him in desire. He began to move hard, taking her hips in his arm, his mouth on hers, grinding his lips against hers, needing her flesh, and she clung to him until he came over the edge and fell down the long precipice with a great groan.

She looked at him. He was still slumbering like a baby. She smiled. She put the sleeping pills back in the cabinet, poured the rest of the champagne down the sink and rinsed the bottle. He'd be out all night.

She undressed him and took her lace stretch panties and her garter stockings and put them on him. The fit was very snug, but it just looked even sexier. A little eye shadow, mascara and her red lipstick. This was quite fun. He was intensely alluring, strangely erotic even, and she let her hand linger, stroking the sexy bulge under the lace. He moved slightly and she reluctantly removed her hand.

She got her phone and took several photos from various angles. She made sure the newspaper with the date was in them, along with the hotel's logo. She uploaded them to her computer and filed them under 'Was it Good for You?' Who could say where they might leak out to?

He was tempting, all the delicious hard beauty of him. Before she cleaned him up, dressed him and called housekeeping to take him back to his room, there was time. She kissed his ruby lips. Then she sat by him, propped up against the pillows, her legs spread, and ran one hand over the muscles of his smooth chest.

Her mind began a downward spiral of swirling coloured lights, like the credits of a bad Seventies movie.

Singapore-based Dawn Farnham is the author of three historical novels set in Singapore, *The Red Thread*, *The Shallow Seas* and *The Hills of Singapore*, published by Monsoon Books, and an Asian-based children's book, *Fan Goes to Sea*, published by Beanstalk Press, Kuala Lumpur. She is working on a crime fiction series set in Western Australia, as well as several screenplays, for which she has received grants from the Singapore Film Commission. Website: *www.dawnfarnham.com*.

Big Love

Chris Mooney-Singh

And so I was left there sitting opposite June. 'Well, this is strangest business trip I've been on,' I said.

'I told you Gerald, you are on holiday. Don't worry. Mr Wang will sign your paperwork before you leave.'

'What do you know about my paperwork?' I queried.

'He makes. You buy. Right? Look, I don't know, Gerald. Mr Wang has many business interests all over Asia. But I have known Mr Wang for a long time and known how he works with people. This is his style when he likes someone. He likes you.'

I must admit I had felt flattered or relieved hearing that, but still I still had my distrusting Singaporean guard up.

Instead I said, 'Hmmm ... really.'

'Look, Gerald, relax! Enjoy yourself. Is that so hard?' she laughed this time with a feeling of tired wisdom. 'Look, I will tell you straight, Gerald. Mr Wang has been good to me over the years. Yes, there is love there, but he also lets me be myself. I am *haenyo*, after all, under all this lard.' She laughed more freely, then reached across and squeezed my hand, asking, 'Gerald, tell me the truth. So do you like me a little bit? Or am I just the boss' fat girl you have to spend some time with?'

The more I had seen of June, the more I found her smart, refreshing and quite unpretentious. Perhaps not being a typical 'sex-goddess' in society's eyes had made someone like June come from a more sincere place. She had the gift of putting people at ease and was least concerned about herself. There was humility and loveliness in that. After seeing those hefty women divers, she had also taken on a new aura of big woman status in my mind also, a kind I had not allowed myself to appreciate before.

'You have a lovely face, a lovely nature, June. And I saw how much effort you put into making Mr Wang happy. Alright, you are full-size, but only a large body could house such a big heart,' and I squeezed her hand back.

'Oh, you're sweet!' And with that, she lunged forward, grabbing me by each cheek with the flats of her strong hands and pulled me directly into the soft vastness of her bosom, kissing me wet on the lips. Then, the slippery muscle of her tongue deftly searched inside for my mine, which she located with loving ease, eager to coax, tame and relax it. I felt myself slipping under waves and being dragged by the current into the weedy depths.

But then, I pulled back, remembering who and where I was. This was all a bit too sudden. My God! I was a married man, an unhappy one, yet still married. So, I withdrew, crabwise, my heart still beating forward toward her.

'You're shy.' She laughed. 'Don't worry. This is my nature. I am very friendly. By the way, Mr Wang and I noticed you haven't been eating. You don't seem to like Korean food much, so he wants me to cook for you tonight.'

'No, no, no, no. Please don't trouble yourself. I'm fine. Really.'

'I can't let you go hungry.'

'Really, I don't eat a lot. I work out at the gym with my wi— '

'Your wife? Is she skinny or big like me?'

I realized, I had opened up an area best not gone into.

'Well, she's slim, I guess. A bit obsessed, actually.'

She sensed my discomfort again. 'Don't worry, Gerald. I am not going to come chasing after you to Singapore. What happens in Jeju, stays in Jeju. Just relax.' Again she disarmed me with that fresh, chubby smile.

'Look, if I don't follow Mr Wang's instructions and cook for you, I might lose my job. Would you want that?'

'No. Of course not.'

'Fine then. Glad we got that out of the way!'

'But ...'

'Shssh ... look, I have to rush now and arrange for Mr Wang and his guests. He doesn't like it when instructions are not followed closely. I'll be back. Just sit tight. Enjoy. Put on the limo TV, have another beer. Oh, and by the way, I'm thinking pasta. I make good pasta.'

'Yes, but ...'

'No buts!' she admonished me firmly, shaking her finger in a friendly way. 'I'll be right back. Don't go anywhere.'

She spoke something in Korean to the driver over the phone intercom, got out, then strode forcefully into the hotel.

* * *

I hadn't expected this. I now remembered again how dumbfounded and totally stupid I had felt. At such times, fear and doubt prey on the mind. You question everyone's intentions. I had wondered what Wang was up to. He had nothing to gain from me. I needed *his* business, not the other way around. Truly, it was very odd. I had never met such a strange entrepreneur before in all the fifteen years of my working life. Why such generosity? No one does things for no reason. My suspicious Singapore brain was working overtime. Who in their right mind would be doing all this for me?

But the more I asked, the more I found that I had no real logical answers. Putting the pieces together, I saw that June had clearly been Wang's employee in the hotel and casino. Was he the silent owner? Why hadn't he let on and how had June come to be here as his aide de camp?

Yes, I had gotten myself into a real state, feeling impatient and upset, thinking that perhaps he was avoiding talking business because he was not going to give me the contract after all. Perhaps he was letting me down gently. I was booked to leave the very next day. Should I trust what June said—that he liked me and would definitely sign the deal? I sighed and really prayed that she was right.

Remembering all those fears and uncertain emotions while waiting in the limousine had made me resolve: *Hang it, Gerald. Stop being such a wimp. Just let things happen or you end up with an ulcer.* That's how I had slapped myself around for awhile sitting in this millionaire's long black piece of luxury on four wheels, parked outside a huge hotel with its own flashing casino in the basement. Thus, I had reached for another Hite beer from the car-bar, switched to the other seat, pressed the console button that opened a compartment to a mini limo TV and channel-surfed: a children's game show with the host dressed like a bear, a Korean cooking segment of the news with a local personality. I then sunk down in the seat with some dated Hollywood action flick dubbed in Korean with the ads scrolled along the bottom of the screen in block-character Korean, gulping my beer. It only took a moment and I began to feel drowsy. Yes, it was true I had hardly eaten a thing that day, starting with a disturbed breakfast and now the beer was going straight to my head. My eyelids and head began to droop.

I don't know how long I nodded off for, but as the limo door opened I sat up, startled to see her back. This time, she plonked herself down with a heavy bounce next to me, closed the door, gave instructions to the driver through the intercom and then looked directly into my eyes, as if knowing that I was feeling awkward and uncomfortable. She took my head very gently like a baby and rested me on her ample bosom.

'There, relax,' she said in a very soothing voice as she stroked my hair. As if going under hypnosis, I just followed instructions and let my last guard drop.

I must have gone straight to sleep again. When I woke up, I was brought to consciousness by June's voice:

'Here we go.'

She was easing me out of the cab, up stairs, into a lift, supporting me with her strong ample body that was like a soft vertical sofa. Was I leaning up or lying down? I couldn't tell. The chime of the lift bell startled me.

'Where am I?'

'Home,' she said, sliding a key into the lock and bouncing back the door with her sneaker as she navigated me inside. The light went on and I saw a comfortable apartment with a white, U+-shaped sofa that looked vaguely familiar.

She deposited me there. I put my phone on the coffee table.

'There, Baby. Give me a moment.'

Directly in front was a huge aquarium with all kinds of colourful fish, rocks and weed waving in the electro-generated current. Yes, I thought, this was just about right for the home of a *haenyo*.

June came back from the bedroom or wherever and bounced herself down beside me with a towel and bathrobe.

'Here. Go take a shower. You'll feel much better.' And then kissed me again, hugging me close to the warm and abundant coastline of herself. This time, I responded with my tongue. She allowed me to explore her mouth and, then broke off.

'Ah we are now waking up, are we?' And with that, kissed me again with a quick smacking sound, rousing and pushing me off in the direction of the bathroom.'

'Go on!'

I went in, closed the door, undressed, relieved myself and then lingered under the hot water and let my thoughts drift for quite a while. Yes, I was definitely in the hands of a big, loving woman. I heard her voice echoing in my mind: *Just relax*. One sucking kiss had brought on my first penile wetness in the cab and now here, thinking of it under the water, I had become hard. I tried to control myself with neutral thoughts and, fearing that I would come then and there, I got out of the shower, towelled myself dry and put on the red bathrobe, tying it around the middle. I slicked back my wet hair with the comb from my back pocket, looked in the mirror, took a deep breath, then returned to the living room.

She had dimmed the lighting and some jazz was playing on the DVD player. I took my position again on the couch. There were cooking smells coming from the kitchen area that formed one side of the living room separated by a bench and bar stools. I smelled boiling water, salt, herbs and tomatoes and there was the sound of chopping. I didn't look over my shoulder. I had decided to let things unfold and accept whatever dish of experience was offered.

'Feeling better?'

'Tremendous,' I said lounging back into the sofa.

'Almost ready,' she said. I heard the ping of a microwave and also the opening and closing of a fridge door. In a moment she was coming to join me, humming something in Korean to herself, holding a tray: on it were three small white bottles and two small ceramic cups. There were also various pickles, seaweeds and something hot—pancake squares with all kinds of vegetables cooked into them. She must have had a supply and quickly microwaved them. There was also a kimchi for good measure, which still smelled like detergent. Some things one never gets used to. She poured with the right hand, while holding the elbow with her left, then passed me the bottle. The liquor was milky-white.

'Now you pour for me,' she said. Being left-handed, I transferred the plastic bottle.

'No, no. The Korean way,' she said, re-positioning it in my right with my left just below the elbow as she had done. It seemed strange, but seeing that I had decided to surrender to whatever came, I accepted her direction and filled her cup.

'We always pour for each other. It is polite.'

'That's nice,' I said.

Now she picked up her wine cup with two hands, nodding for me to do the same.

'Both poised and ready, she said 'One shot!' indicating for us to down our drinks at the same time.

The drink was both sweet and sour, almost rough and raw and she was quickly refilling for me, and I for her.

'This is really nice,' I said, 'the best thing I've tried in Korea, by far.'

'Makgeolli was a farmer's drink. It's beer. Made from mixed grains and fermented; it gives *strength*,' She laughed, I guess wondering whether I got her joke. 'Ah, you just need a good guide.'

'Thankfully, I have found one,' and looked straight at her.

'Yes, you have,' she giggled. 'Okay, now we play!'

With that, she deftly undid the soft belt around my bathrobe and found my penis, already hardening in her chubby little palms. Then she kneeled between my legs and took me in her mouth, working my shaft into the mollusk of her mouth, bringing her tongue to bear, on occasion, from root to cock-head; and soon she changed her strategy of arousal by putting the whole of my scrotal sac into her mouth and rolling the testicles around like small, hard-boiled eggs.

'Mmmm,' she said and then worked me harder and faster. Already aroused from the shower, I couldn't hold myself back any longer and came prematurely with a loud release, jetting my load between her lips.

'Mmmm,' I heard her say again, sitting up now before me and swilling my viscous whiteness around in her mouth, giggling and making eyes at me, letting some dribble out the side and then playfully pushing it back in with a finger. Then, without swallowing, she put her powerful arms around my neck and kissed me with the mouth full of my own cum. The residue of the white rice beer in my mouth merged with that taste of semen. I had never tried anything like this before. It was indescribable. My wife, Pearl Lin, would have died of shock.

June passed the load into my mouth and followed with her tongue sucking it back and forth, giving and taking, giving and taking—her pink tongue moving like a sea worm in our salty current. It grew in volume with our saliva, the full flavour of those two white essences perfectly matched and mixed now into one white cocktail of human sugars and acids. Then, with the same trademark deftness, she sucked my ejaculate back into her mouth, took ownership of it, so to speak, withdrew from my lips and swallowed it down with a satisfying release.

'Ahhhhh,' she said licking her lips and fingers. 'Thanks for the vitamin pill. So nice. Now you know the secret of my young complexion,' she laughed. 'This is June's own special technique for drinking Korean rice beer,' she said with a slutty twinkle in her eye. 'You like?'

'I like. That was awesome. Come back here!' With that I grabbed, but despite her dimensions, she had easily out-manoeuvred me to the side of the sofa and was now pouring me another cup of the milky beer. I took her cue and did the same for her.

'One shot!' We both said, and holding each cup with two hands, drained our drinks.

'Now I must check on dinner and I will take my little shower. Okay?'

'Sure. Please.'

Yes, I was in the hands of a big Korean sea-nymph who was kind, creative and sexier than I could ever imagine. After the entrée, I wondered what was coming next.

The jazz played on in the background and it seemed that the fish in the aquarium were swimming in sequence to the beat, now turning this way, flashing another direction on cue. Despite the violation of etiquette, I poured myself another cup of rice beer and even picked at the side dishes, trying the pancake slices. *Yes, kind of like a Korean pizza,* I thought, and munched happily on one. I even tried a forkful of the black seaweed and a cube or two of pickled turnip. Downed with the rice beer, they weren't too bad. In fact, they complemented each other. But I still steered clear of the kimchi.

The fish continued their technicolour routines in the aquarium and now I looked around and saw a painting on the wall. It was a portrait of the old *haenyo*.

Wang and June had brought me to see these famous women divers along the Jeju coastline earlier in the day. Her mother had been a diver, and June herself had imbibed from a young age that same trait of fierce independence of the *haenyo*, who didn't rely on husbands to earn a living. I thought this was most unusual in an Asian culture; certainly different from my Singapore upbringing.

I got up to study more closely: Two women were sitting on the rocks. The grandma in the blue one-piece was smoking a cigarette, the other had a white cloth around her loins and was stretching and scratching the back of her head with her magnificent breasts and orange-tipped nipples exposed to the afternoon sunlight. In the background, you could see the green-mesh trap with its orange float and a small trident used to loosen shellfish from underwater cracks and crevices.

They were coarse, Rubenesque, heavy jowled, with almost bulbous red clown noses. Perhaps this was the result of prolonged cold water diving and holding your breath at depth. I looked at the right bottom corner of the painting. There was a name or inscription written in Korean and a date: 1956.

I couldn't help myself, so I found my phone and took a picture of the painting. It was so beautiful, and June Park could be found in every centimetre of it.

I felt as if I was swimming in the sea and moved and swayed in time with the jazz and the fish, until the next pleasant surprise of the evening: June had bathed and there she was dressed in traditional Korean red-and-white costume with her hair made up. I had seen photos of this courtly garb before, but had not realized that it really was a 'fat' dress. The red blouse at the top came up just under her breast-line and the skirt fanned out conically below into a wide circumference touching the floor.

'Wow, June!'

She giggled and moved as if on invisible dolly-wheels in my direction.

'Let me take your picture,' I said, positioning and snapping her from various angles and in different poses—some serious, some girly, some comical, some down and dirty. She was so connected to her feelings that she was a natural model. I took some near the back-lit lampshade, another in the bedroom doorway, one looking out the high-rise window and others near the colourfully lit aquarium.

'What can I say? This dress ... It's so ... you, June!'

'So now, Mr Singapore, this is my present—gift-wrapped in my traditional Korean *hang-bok*. Am I pretty?'

'Pretty? You are gorgeous!' and I meant it. She had really brought me to that point of appreciation for unpretentious pleasure and a belief in the importance of living lustfully in the moment. We joined lips and embraced for a long time with the oxygen filter gurgling in the background.

Primed and confident, I now felt it was my turn to give and not just receive. I was ready to fold back her inner sound of fabric and started by running my hands down her red-necked blouse over its breast-points, so elegantly and classically tailored with all the grace-lines of

Korean history and ceremony intact. Then, I knelt to find her hidden ankles and kissed them.

She then helped by turning around and bending over, spread legs wide, while gripping the back of the sofa seat. She knew what she wanted. I put my hands underneath and lifted outer silk and inner petticoat, finding fleshy hand-holds and wet dew trickling down the inside of her thighs. I was soon rubbing my two palms up warm flesh and feasting my eyes on the curvature of her dimpled buttocks, scored with life-accumulated cellulite as if they were star-indents of real experience and accomplishment, not the bane of some prurient weight-watcher's programme. Yes, she was most un-Hollywood, an unabashedly dimpled daughter of the sea, a traveller's insulation against cold days and lonely nights. She was ever-prepared for picnic or camper fun, carrying like a small jumbo—her own howdah of excess baggage.

In the overwhelming presence of Big, I wondered why thin was so sought after today? I now realized how more comfortable it was to ride a fleshy she-mammal, rather than fearing you might crush some bony sea-horse with an exposed skeleton, like Pearl Lin.

But it wasn't just about size or dimension. Desire was clearly a set of guided responses, manufactured and cultivated by aesthetics that differed from place to place around the globe and were also different during other periods of history. The ample body of June Park from Jeju-do now made me realize that life was meant to be big, broad-minded and ever-generous, not skinny, calculating and mean-hearted.

She bent over more to let me moisten her crevice with saliva, yet there was no need. She had already thoughtfully applied lubricant and I found myself hardening again, ready to caress the rosy petals of this Everywoman's lower mouth.

Instinctive as a diver, I entered carefully, my member raised like a shellfish trident, the tool used to prise loose the pearl of an arching clitoris. I fitted and rode her standing, working the hump-backed mammal into deep water, riding the wave of our lust without fear of failing, until I came to the precipice of climax and withdrew, controlling myself a little, then flipping her over like the underside of a ribbed crayfish. Her silk-dressed back now skewered gently to the top of the sofa chair, I opened her legs gently again, exploring wet loins up to her waist with hands carefully spreading the silk and petticoat cotton. Then, down-kneeling, I kissed and tongued the red anemone within that sea-crevice, finding her taste as authentic as the brine of the sea.

I stood and entered again, from the front now, looking into her eyes which met mine equally and with happiness as I thrust again and again, fully fountaining, releasing my milky beer and merging guttural *yeses* with the reciprocal moans she was uttering.

If a man has limits, these are not found in a woman who can still ache on for an interminable time, imploring her diver to go deeper and deeper. I tried and tried and then failed happily, until there was nothing left of my white blow to eke out for either of us. Spent, I lay across her like an octopus, limp on a hoard of sea-catch, joined to the mother-lode and a larger sense of the globe than what I had previously allowed myself to experience. As I came back to consciousness, I felt her arms like soft feelers at my back. The lit aquarium continued to gurgle and the fish schools did their jazz-jive to DVD music in the background.

'June. I feel incredible.' We came back to the couch.

'This *hang-bok* was my mother's,' she said. It's special. I don't really wear it much. It's mainly for special occasions, but tonight I wanted to wear it for you. Even Wang hasn't seen it.'

I felt special. 'I will always treasure this,' I said. Then she poured me more Mokgeolli. I now realized why this ritual was done with the right hand holding the bottle and left hand on the elbow. This was clearly to make sure the *hang-bok*'s sleeve didn't drip into the wine cup.

'Actually, it is a bit old and delicate. I never made love with it on before. I thought it would be a fun idea, something a sensitive man like you would appreciate. But let me go and take it off now. Okay?'

With that, she disappeared into the bedroom. I sat there feeling pleased with myself so I took another slice of the pizza-pancake and washed it down with wine.

Soon she was back wearing a matching bathrobe. 'You must be hungry' she said. I nodded, but to tell the truth, I was fully satiated on a deeper level. It didn't matter now whether or not I ate food.

'Let me finish the pasta.' She did her work quite quickly and allowed me to mind-drift for a while.

'Hey, I recognize this furniture. Is it from Wang's warehouse?'

'Yes, it is. A gift.' She didn't say more.

Before long, she had brought two steaming mountains of curlicue pasta with sauce, made room on the table and then proceeded to put the first few forkfuls into my mouth. After getting me lovingly started, she proceeded with her own and began to eat with concentration. We didn't talk, but she looked up from time to time to smile at me.

Dinner done, I tried to get up and clear the plates, but she shook her head. 'Leave them,' and dumped mine on top of hers at the end of the coffee-table.

'Let's drink,' she said. We poured again for each other, said 'One shot' and downed our cups … again and again.

From then on, we passed the night hardly speaking but nestled together in our matching robes, watching the dance of the pretty fish and becoming tipsier and tipsier until I passed out on her shoulder.

I woke mid-morning and found myself nestled nakedly against an equally naked mountain. She had somehow transferred me to her bed and she was still snoring lightly beside me. I pulled back the sheet and looked at the whole side of her bulging body. She looked beautiful, still.

Beauty, I thought, is just a mental construction of emotions felt for its object. Beauty shifts and changes like weather, according to the eye of the beholder. Beauty is electricity lighting the lamp and illuminating the fish tank. I would never be able to think of a fat person in the old light again, I realized, and ran my hand over her rump to reassure myself that this realization was indeed real and would last.

The touch of my hand climbing up and down June's sleeping coastline began to tickle her and, suddenly, she woke with a start.

'Oh, Gerald, are you still here? What happened? What time is it?'

'I think we've overslept.' There was a digital alarm clock on my side of the bed. 'It's 11.45.'

'What? Mr Wang will kill me! What time is your flight?'

'One-thirty,' I answered.

'Hurry up. Get dressed. We must go to the hotel and pack your things.'

'Don't worry,' I said, 'I could stay on a day longer.'

'No, no. You cannot. Mr Wang is not available. You must get up.

We have to get your papers signed, remember?'

Conscience struck. 'Oh yes, the contract. I had completely forgotten that.'

'Quick now. Jump in the shower.' Reluctantly I obeyed orders, showered and shaved when I saw an electric razor there, and then splashed on some cologne from June's shelf.

Chris Mooney-Singh is a full-time writer, publisher and literary worker. The recipient of several grants from Singapore's National Arts Council, he has travelled to many international festivals and events. Mooney-Singh co-edited *The Penguin Book of Christmas Poems* (Penguin Books Australia) and his last two books were *The Taxi Buddha Cab Company* and *The Bearded Chameleon*. Recently returned to play and fiction writing, four of his short stories were featured in *Best of Singapore Erotica*, *Love and Lust in Singapore* and *Crime Scene: Singapore* published by Monsoon Books. *Big Love* is excerpted from an unpublished story of the same name.

Closely Watched Dreams

Zafar Anjum

When the clock struck six, Alvin lifted his fingers off the keyboard, threw a glance at the wall clock and got up from his seat. Today, he was too excited to waste a single minute after putting in exactly eight hours at work—if his supervisor was keeping an eye on him, so be it. He was done with his duty for the day. Now, it was time for pleasure.

The reason for his excitement was a CD-ROM in his bag that he had just burned off the Web. It contained a rare video game that had been pulled off the shelves in Tokyo and was now internationally banned. His friend Keigo in Japan, who had bought the game from Akihibara before it was banned, had managed to send him a copy via the Net.

'Enjoy!' That was all Keigo had written in his email message.

'You cryptic coder, I love you, bastard!' he had written back. The two geeks had met at an Internet conference in Tokyo five years ago and had stayed in touch with each other ever since—Alvin had hosted him in Singapore when he had come on a visit three years ago, and then the two of them had a short *mancation* in Phuket. They enjoyed each other's company as they shared many common interests.

'Enjoy!' Keigo had advised and that was exactly what he intended to do after reaching home. The beautiful thing was that the coast was clear for him; *pleasure is ensured when providence conspires in your favour*, Alvin thought with a chuckle.

His wife Juliana, who worked with a PR firm, had called earlier in the day. 'Darling, I'll be late from work,' she had said.

'How late?'

'It could be eight, nine, in that vicinity,' she had said. That was good news for him, he thought, suppressing his giggles.

'Something unusual, honey?' he asked, sounding serious.

'We're handling the launch of a new mobile phone.'

'Oh, I see,' he said and went silent for a minute. 'Another smartphone, huh? Which company?'

'Asus.'

'The Taiwanese one?'

'Yah, lor.'

Alvin and Juliana had met through a common friend at a party, had instantly taken to each other and after dating for two years, had tied the knot. That was four years ago.

The first few months of marriage were blissful—honeymoon in Tokyo and Kyoto and uncountable moments of intimacy. But after some time, their interest in each other had dwindled and slowly he had slipped back into his dark world of dorky carnality, each night fantasizing and pleasuring himself with a different girl online.

In real life, husband and wife hardly had sex more than once or twice a month. But that didn't bother Alvin as he knew his score was close to the national average: Singaporeans were not ardent love-makers. He remembered reading a survey report by a condom company in *Today* which put his countrymen near the bottom of the frequency list.

'No problem, darling,' he said to his wife. 'Take your time, sweet love. Ciao!'

Alvin switched off his computer, slung the strap of his black bag across his shoulder, and, tossing an indifferent 'see you guys tomorrow' at his colleagues who were still bent over their computers, stepped out of the office.

The elevator made several stops on its way down from the thirtieth floor. By the time the elevator had completed half its descent, it got packed with bodies young and old, and Alvin chose to stare at the cleavage of a busty Indian girl with chunky thighs.

'Ding!' the elevator squealed and its doors flung open as people rushed out. He followed the Indian girl and took pleasure in watching the sway of her hips. He yearned to see her face once more, so he let out a muffled wolf whistle; the girl turned back to look at him. Their eyes met, she made a pouting face and marched on, all the while maintaining her composure. Her look of disgust did not bother him—he moved on without a care in the world, whistling to himself.

Outside, the day was bright and clear, the sun on its last leg of the afternoon. It had rained in the afternoon, so the square outside his office and the road that led off the square to the bus stand were rain-drenched and shiny. Even though it was March, there was a slight nip in the air that pleased Alvin, making his skin bristle under his T-shirt.

Manoeuvering his way through the rain-filled puddles, he

reached the bus stand. It didn't take long for his bus to arrive. But before that, he gawked at the girls at the bus stop. He disrobed some of them with his mind's eye and was pleased to see what he saw. *Wish I had those long legs wrapped around me*, he thought, looking at a tall, well-proportioned Chinese girl.

He got down from the bus at a market near his apartment, stepped into a food court and had a bowl of beef noodles. Sitting among many working people eating their dinner, he saw some families having their dinner—their tables filled with trays of food, colourful school bags and water bottles.

He saw a toddler whining, refusing to eat what his parents had bought for him. The distraught parents were trying to make him see reason. He felt a renewed disgust for children. 'Tiny little runts.'

Alvin hated kids—they signified to him an end to his independence, not to mention the danger to the environment that they posed. First marriage and then children—how low can a man fall, he used to think. Marriage he could not help, because one needed a partner to buy an HDB flat in Singapore. That was the law. But he was decidedly against having babies and had told his wife so. Walking home, he felt an unusual spring in his feet; the excitement of the new porn game waiting to be played made him drool with anticipation.

When he reached his apartment, he found his wife at home, splayed before the TV on the three-piece black leather sofa, sipping a Starbucks latte.

'What the fuck?' he muttered.

'What happened, honey?' he said, tossing his bag on the sofa. 'You said you would be late.'

'Why?' his wife teased him, lowering the volume of the home theatre system. 'Not happy to see me home?'

'No, lah ...' he mumbled. 'I didn't mean that ...'

'The event ended earlier than expected,' she said, running fingers through her hair, trying to smile. 'I had a splitting headache, and my boss let me go home.'

'Well,' he replied, 'You did the right thing. Better take rest then.'

'Yeah.'

'Want me to put some Tiger Balm on your— '

'No need, no need. I've taken a Panadol. And now this latte.'

'Okay, lah. As you wish.'

Now that his plan had gone awry (he imagined the CD sitting in his bag in a melancholy pose), he needed some distraction.

'Dinner?' she said, looking askance at him, her face towards him at an angle from the 42-inch Sony Bravia.

'Had mine,' he said. 'You?'

'Don't feel like eating anything.'

'Sure?'

'Yeah,' she said and upped the volume of the TV. 'I will finish the coffee and crash. Want some?' she added, holding up the coffee cup in her hands, her eyes on the screen.

'No thanks,' he said, smiling at her. 'I've got to freshen up.' He sucked his cheeks and went inside the bathroom. Alvin found the bathroom tiles cold under his feet. He stood still for a moment, enjoying the coolness, then turned the water heater on. He took off his clothes and hung them on a peg on the door. Naked, he stood facing the bathroom mirror in which he could see his face and half his torso. He went a few steps back and now he could see the lower end of his tummy and his waist.

He was young and broad-shouldered in the image, but he could see his little paunch, disfiguring his V-shape. He put both his hands over the flab on his belly and gathered it. He felt the fat underneath his skin with his fingers. Then he turned sideways and looked again at himself in the mirror. He sucked in his stomach and admired his youthful posture in the reflection. The bathroom door was open. Juliana peeped inside. A beat of silence, then he asked: 'How's your headache?'

'Feeling much better now. The pill is working— '

'Good.' She kept on standing at the door and examined him head to toe. Looking into his eyes sensually, she reached out and ran her fingers over his bare chest. Then she ran the back of her hand over his lips. He gently kissed her fingers. Before turning back, she smiled and said, 'I'll finish the movie and then try to sleep.'

'What are you watching?'

'*Inglourious Basterds*. My colleague Margaret gave it to me.'

'I'll join you after the shower?'

She said 'okay' and went away. He pissed into the toilet bowl, washed his hands and then turned the shower on. The lukewarm water felt good on his skin.

After the bath, he dried himself with a towel, walked into his bedroom and put on boxer shorts and a T-shirt. He felt neat and fresh.

Juliana was still sitting on the couch, her eyes glued to the TV screen. A scene with Hitler holding a meeting was on. He stood behind her, his arms curled over her stomach, his chin on her shoulder, close to her nape. He kissed her cheek and pressed his face into hers, smelling her familiar Chanel No. 5 fragrance. 'Honey, you finish the movie and come to sleep,' he murmured to her, moving away. 'Enjoy the movie; I'm going to lie down inside.' He wanted her to sleep early.

'Okay, darling,' she said, without taking her eyes off the screen.

He went into the bedroom, lay on the bed and started turning the pages of a book of short stories by Isaac Asimov that he'd been reading. He began reading a story that he had dog-eared, but got bored after a few paragraphs. Feeling sleepy, he put the book down on the side table, closed his eyes and drifted off. After a while, he woke up, thinking of the CD that he was yet to try. 'Juliana' he called his wife out. There was no response.

He emerged from the bedroom. The movie had ended; Juliana was fast asleep on the sofa. She looked calm and her face glistened in the pale blue light of the TV screen. Her fleshy eyelids covered her beautiful dark eyes. 'Juliana,' he whispered. She didn't move. Then he shook her by her shoulder.

'Ah, sorry, I fell asleep, didn't I?' she sat up and smiled, rubbing her eyes with her hands. 'I had a dream. A funny little dream,' she added, smiling. Her eyes looked drunk.

'What did you dream?' he said, leaning on her.

She said, 'You sure want to hear it?'

'Yeah,' he replied.

'Later, when we go to sleep, okay? I'm feeling hungry now,' she said, gently pushing him aside. After she had eaten, he cleaned the table and put away the used plates. Juliana came into the bedroom with a bottle of water. Laying it on her bedside table, she turned off the light and spread herself on the bed. A patch of light came into the room from across the neighbour's bathroom window. She lay still for a minute in a relaxed posture. Alvin turned over his side toward her and took her in his arms. He squeezed her back gently. 'Tell me about the dream, honey,' he said. 'Well, I told you it was a little dream. I can't remember everything in it now, but what I do remember is that I saw you with a woman.'

'A woman? What woman? Where?'

'It was a scenic place, a beach perhaps. She was in a bikini. She was running ahead of you and you were chasing after her.'

'And where were you?' he said, looking into her eyes.

'I don't remember. I'm not sure if I was there at all,' she said, sounding distant. '

And who was that woman? Do you remember that?'

She spoke slowly. 'A tall and slim young woman. Blonde. Athletic figure. Her face has kind of faded away from my memory. She wore a red bikini. Like one of those girls in *Baywatch*.'

He laughed. She twitched her lips. He raised up on his elbows and brought his face close to hers. 'You are jealous of her, aren't you honey?' he said.

'I don't know,' she said.

He laughed again. She had her eyes closed now. He kissed her lips. She lay still. 'What's the matter, Juliana?' he said.

'My legs hurt, especially the thighs. I wish you'd rub them,' she said.

'Gosh,' he said gently. 'Why didn't you tell me before?'

'You must be tired yourself,' she said. She had a pleading look in her eyes.

'Tch,' he clucked his tongue. He sat on the bed and began

pressing her legs. He began from the feet and went up to the hips. She sighed while he rubbed her legs. The muscles on her hip felt supple. He bent down and kissed her feet. She wiggled her toes playfully. He ran his fingers on her heels. 'Ah,' she moaned with pleasure and her legs shivered. When he put his hand inside her nightie, he could feel the goose pimples on her skin. He turned her over on her back. Lifting her jumper, he kissed her navel and dug his tongue's tip into it. She raised up her hips and let out a sigh. His tongue travelled up to her bosom. He took the nipples in his mouth, one after another, and sucked them. Her bosom heaved. 'One second,' she said, sitting up. She removed her nightie and went back to the old pose. When he moved his hand over her groin, her bottom swelled. She parted her legs and when he touched her there, he found that she was wet. He got out of his shorts and entered her with eagerness. She sighed with pleasure as he went deep inside her. She gaped with her eyes wide open in rapture. When he was about to come, he asked her to straddle him. While she was on top of him, he squeezed her breasts, tickled her nape. Then he cupped her face with his hands.

'Juliana,' he said.

'Yeah,' she breathed heavily.

'Honey, say something kinky,' he said.

'Like what?'

'Like anything. Maybe a fantasy. You know what I mean, honey,' he said.

'I don't have any fantasies. But I know you have,' she said. He gave her a quizzical look. Her strokes were stronger and more rapid now. She looked beautiful as her mane bobbed along with

241

her heaving bosoms. 'I know you want to fornicate with other women,' she said.

'How can you say that?'

'Don't ask me, dear. I just know.'

A strong tingle overwhelmed him. He felt it wouldn't be long before he came.

'You can,' she said.

'What?' he said, his body tense, blood throbbing in his veins.

'Sleep with them, if you want,' she said.

'How would you take that, honey?'

'No probs.' He could not believe his ears. He held her by the hips and helped her in the motions. 'Come again?' he asked her.

'I said no objections.' She was moving up and down on him aggressively, enjoying the congress. He knew she would climax soon.

'Can't believe this. Carte blanche. No caveats whatsoever, hon?' he managed to say.

'Fuck them and forget them,' she said. 'No friendship, no relationship with the whores. That I couldn't take.'

A couple of female faces he fancied reeled before his eyes, including the Indian girl in the office lift and the tall Chinese girl at the bus stand. He imagined them naked, riding on top of him. For a moment, he saw them, one by one, replacing Juliana's face. She humped him harder. She shook her head and swiftly put her hand on his mouth. She craned her neck upwards and came, crying with ecstasy. Her movement ceased like an engine cut. He held her hair in a tight grasp and, at about the same time, he came too, drenching him in a wave of pleasure.

He heard his heart pump hard and he could feel blood throb under his flesh. She tightened her muscles around him and, feeling the action, he smiled at her. She bent over him and kissed him on the lips. 'I love you,' she said. 'I love you too,' he said. He took her in his arms. Then she lay still on his chest, quietly, taking small breaths. A few minutes passed like this. He listened to the sounds their bodies made while they began to cool down. His stomach growled, making him wince. The wall clock ticked loudly. He heard their neighbours flush the toilet.

Outside, a car rubbered by on the road. A plane flew over the apartment, its noise filled the air for a minute. He felt his throat parch. He freed his body from hers. With a groan, she turned onto her back, her eyes closed, relaxed. He pulled a sheet on her body. She seemed to sleep like a baby. Her face glowed with innocence and sensuality. He heard someone running the tap in the apartment next door. A dog barked somewhere in the neighbourhood. The tap was turned off.

'Juliana,' he whispered.

There was no answer. He climbed out of the bed and put on his clothes. Then he went into the bathroom and washed himself. He sprinkled water on his hair, took a comb and parted his hair from the middle. Then he parted his hair from the side. Then he slicked it back. He didn't find any of the hairstyles to his liking.

He came out of the bathroom waltzing with an imaginary beauty. A brunette—tall, slim, and athletic; she wore a splendid red dress. He imagined himself in a black tuxedo. They danced on the floor for a while. After a time, they stopped dancing and started kissing each other.

He sat down on a dining chair and she sat down beside him, cross-legged. He could see her juicy thighs through the slit of her skirt. He lit a cigarette and offered her one. Both of them smoked. Then he asked her to sit on his lap. She obeyed him. He held her by her waist and began whispering sweet nothings in her ear.

'Alvin,' Juliana called out to him from the bedroom.

'Yes, honey,' he said, a little loudly. 'You awake?' More than half of his cigarette had burnt. The ashes had fallen on his clothes and on the floor.

'Come on in here. I don't want to be all by myself,' she said.

He took a puff of the cigarette and crushed it in the ashtray. He shook the ash from his clothes and went to the bedroom.

'Where were you?' she asked huskily. She looked groggy.

'In the bathroom,' he lied. He sat by her side. She didn't say anything. He lay on the bed and inched his body closer to her. She put her arm over him and patted him on the chest, indicating that he should sleep. He lay still for some time, listening to his own breaths. Excitedly, he thought about what she had said just a while ago while making love. Was it just to arouse him? If she was serious, he could feel less guilty about his porn-watching habit—in fact, they could watch it together if she wanted.

Did she mean it? More than that, did he want it? He wasn't sure about anything. He wanted to talk to her.

'Juliana? Honey?' There was no response. He tapped his toes against hers.

'Yeah,' she groaned feebly.

'Did you really mean what you said a while ago?' he said. 'That stuff about other women.' There was no answer. She lay huddled against his body, looking angelic in her deep sleep. He shook her shoulder gently. She did not move an inch, nor say a thing. All he could hear was her breathing.

He thought of the new porn game CD in his bag. He thought of sneaking out to his study and playing it on his PC. When he stood up to make a move, Juliana caught his hand.

'Where are you going?'

'To the other room. Wanted to finish some office work.'

'I know why you're going to the other room. To watch porn.'

For a moment he felt as if a tremor had hit the building.

'What are you talking about, Juliana?' he said, her words stinging him.

'Yes; I even know about your 95-dollar-a-month subscription to a porn website,' she said, looking at him intently. 'You are addicted to porn, Alvin. You better admit it.'

'How do you— ' he mumbled, feeling naked and exposed. His face turned pale.

She said, 'Alvin, I am your wife, I know.'

She should have been furious and spiteful, but she was not. She was so calm, he felt like a child in front of her.

'I am sorry, honey,' he said, his voice laden with guilt. 'I am so sorry,' he repeated, not daring to look at her, and shoved his face into her hair. He held her close and kissed her, but she was unmoved, distant. He felt heavy and stuffed inside and began to cry. 'I love you honey, I love you,' he said as he cried.

'I love you, too, Alvin, but you need help, you understand?'

'I think I do,' he said, tears rolling down his cheeks. 'I do need help— '

He nodded his head vigorously, like a schoolboy who had just escaped severe punishment. The two of them remained seated on the bed like a pair of still shadows. The patch of light from the room backed away as the tube across the window was turned off.

Zafar Anjum is a journalist and author and is the editor of Kitaab.org and Writersconnect.org. One of his short stories, *Waiting for the Angels* was a finalist for India's prestigious The Little Magazine New Writing Prize for emerging Indian writers. His stories have been anthologized in Monsoon Books' *Love and Lust in Singapore* (2010) and *Crime Scene: Singapore* (2010). He is one of the recipients of 2010 Arts Creation Fund grant from Singapore's National Arts Council.

I, Teiresius

Alaric Leong

'Yes, they're real.' A pause. 'One hundred percent real.'

Talk about being jolted; I felt like a school kid who'd just been caught doing something naughty in class. I mean, that clarification came from out of nowhere. We had been talking about the advertising industry when suddenly my companion there at the bar had thrown that at me.

'Uhh ... excuse me. I didn't mean to— ' No, I didn't mean to, but the worst thing was that the moment I was accused of it, my eyes automatically slipped down to peer at the things I'd been just sneaking peeks at until then.

She put her hand under my chin and lifted it just a little, to face level.

'My eyes. The colour? This is the real colour of my eyes, this hazel brown. One of my great grandparents was European, from Bohemia or somewhere. I evidently inherited that gene from him.'

'I see. Yes, your eyes. I was ... wondering about that colour. I mean, these days, with all the things you can do, shaded lenses and all.'

'Believe me, I don't have any lenses. I don't need them.'

'That's good to know.'

Then came that sly smile. 'The other things, they're also real. The things you were just sneaking repeated looks at.'

'Excuse me, I didn't— '

'Haven't we been here before? Anyway, to put your doubts to rest: these tits are mine, too.'

'Of course. Who else's would they be?'

And then he ... she ... this strange person sitting opposite me threw his, her head back and gave this husky, deep-throated laugh. Which only deepened my suspicions. Whatever the current status of this woman, I was pretty sure she did not start out life as a female. There were all sorts of clues; that manly laugh was just one of many.

'By the way, what's your full name, Mr Advertising Accounts Executive?'

'Oh, that's right, I didn't ... Raymond Chua.'

'Raymond. Nice name. I've always liked that name. I've often thought that if I have maybe six sons, one of them will definitely be called Raymond.'

'Yeah? Well, like they say, everybody loves Raymond. And your name is ...?'

'Teresa. That's good enough for now. A simple Teresa.'

'But not so simple a person, I think.'

Teresa then crossed her very shapely legs and smiled. 'I court complexities. Simple is, for me, just a synonym for "boring".'

'I see.'

'I hope you don't see! If you did, I wouldn't be complex enough.'

'Okay. Uhh ... can I buy you another drink?'

Teresa nodded. 'I think so. But only if I can buy you a drink in the next round after this one.'

'I wouldn't say "no".' And I didn't.

And so it went for four more rounds, each of us alternating on buying the next round. Her drink was white wine, mine was red. And after that fifth round for both of us, *in vino veritas* had taken command of the conversation. It also produced a certain level of physical comfort. Teresa had already slipped her hand over mine a couple of rounds back, and had now moved it up under my shirt sleeve, lightly stroking the hair on my forearm.

'So ... do you like me, Raymond?'

'I think I do.'

He .. she laughed. 'Why are guys always like that? I wasn't asking who you think is going to win the World Cup. I asked you about your feelings, what you feel. You're not sure what you feel?'

'Well, I ... what I feel is complex. It's ... I don't know how to explain.'

'Okay, Raymond, I do like you. Like you quite a bit. Like you enough to let you ask me.'

'Ask you what?'

'Ask me the question you've been wanting to ask since you first saw me earlier this evening, across the room, when you liked what you saw and then wondered what might be wrong with you for liking it.' There was then a tense pause. 'My sexuality. You're not curious?'

'Sure I am.' I took a deep breath. 'Okay: Teresa, are you really a man?'

Teresa looked me right in the eyes. 'Not anymore.' Bang. Like being hit over the head.

She then inched her left hand over and pulled her plunging neckline down a couple of plunges. 'Like I said, these breasts are real. I had to undergo treatment to grow them, but they are real, they are all Teresa. And Teresa, née David, is now a woman.'

'Do you ... Uhhm, what's the state of your plumbing?'

'Complex. But the main thing is, I don't have a penis. I lost that.'

'Are you a ...'

'Full woman down there? Well, I have a vagina. A functioning vagina.' She then drew a long, sad breath. 'And with that, I think I've just signalled an end to our pleasant conversation this evening. I think I have told you more than I should have told you.' She took her wine glass and rapidly drained the last third. She had the saddest look on her face.

For a moment, I didn't know how to respond, so I just sat there, gazing at her like a fool. 'And you don't have to apologise, Raymond. Or make up some lame excuse. Just tell me that you enjoyed our little intimate chat, but you can't go any further with a woman who grew up a man.'

She sat there, staring off into the corner with a defeated expression. A few moments later, she turned back, managed a loser's smile, then blew me an air kiss, slid off the seat and turned away.

'No, wait,' I called out. 'I'm not turned off by you. In fact, I'm ... I find you even more enticing now that I know the truth.' *In vino veritas* was in full force here.

'Really?'

'Really.'

I didn't tell her, as I should have, that I had long nurtured this fantasy of being with a transsexual. The whole idea of being inside a woman who had once been a man was really a major turn-on. I wanted to know what it was like. In some ways, Teresa was playing right into the core of one of my kinkiest fantasies.

Our conversation then took a sharp turn to the more intimate and more friendly. We each had a half a glass more wine and then decided to take our little party for two to cosier surroundings. I was willing to take her back to my place, but was very glad when she suggested we go to her apartment instead. I was incredibly excited, more than I'd been in a long time. Hell, the moment we stepped out of the club, I was hailing a taxi I spied two streets away.

We held each other tightly in the cab and about halfway back to her place starting kissing rather passionately. I was hoping that the cabbie didn't get a good look at her, but was willing to tell him to go to hell and mind his own business even if he did. I had taken this big step and wasn't going to turn around now.

Back at her place, she offered me another drink, but I decided I didn't need any more alcohol at that point, so just asked for a large glass of water. While I was drinking, Teresa said she wanted to step into the other room for just a few minutes.

When she emerged again, she was wearing a kimono. 'It's genuine, from Kobe. An old boyfriend bought it for me.'

'Oh, that was nice of the old boyfriend.'

'And when I say old, I mean old; he had at least 25 years on me, this guy. But he was so sweet and so intelligent. He was a financial analyst, but we liked to discuss literature together. He was incredibly well-read. I really liked him.'

Back at the bar, Teresa had told me that she was a Lit major at university; NUS, in fact. I never cared all that much for literature, so I quickly steered the discussion off in another direction.

We ended up talking about the standard things, starting with where we grew up, where we went to school, all that duty conversation stuff. But with Teresa, it somehow came out relevant and even interesting.

At one point in our conversation, Teresa loosened the cord on her kimono and opened it slightly. 'Do you know that for traditionalists, it is considered very crass to wear anything under the kimono. Anything at all.'

I suddenly realized how wildly aroused I had become. 'I see. And are you a traditionalist? I wouldn't have thought so.'

'I am in some things. Very much so.' She smiled this very warm smile. It was almost unbearable. God, did I want to get close to her. 'In other ways, I'm not at all traditional.' Then that carefully poised smile again. 'I told you I was complex.'

At this point, in the half-light of the room, I also realized how beautiful Teresa was—in a complex way. Sure, I was attracted to her from almost the moment I saw her, but this was a special kind of beauty which you only see after some time.

From her looks, and also from a few clues she had dropped into the conversation, I determined that in addition to that Bohemian ancestor, she also enjoyed a mixed pedigree of Chinese, Malay and probably even a bit of Indian. Maybe some of the other ASEAN members as well. And it all came together in a strange symphony of stunning features.

We continued kicking around various subjects for maybe another half hour. During this time, she fiddled with the opening of the kimono, occasionally edging it open slowly, then pulling it back together. Finally, at one point, as if it were the most natural thing in the world to do, Teresa pulled the flaps apart, threw her head back like she was posing for a fashion shoot and let the kimono slip off to her sides.

Her beautifully sculpted breasts were tastefully displayed. I couldn't believe how perfect they looked, how ... real. I punched myself mentally. Of course, they were real, she said they were real. Just a little ... late in coming.

Even more interesting to me was that feature a bit south of the breasts. The pussy looked somewhat strange, but pussies can look strange. It also looked real. One thing I noticed was that there wasn't a lot of fuzz covering it. It was almost as if she had shaved it and the hair hadn't fully grown back yet.

I think she read my thoughts, because just as I was thinking about this interesting feature, Teresa deftly moved her hand down there and started stroking slowly. I couldn't believe it. Until that moment, I was even wondering if I would get to realize my long-time fantasy that evening. Now it was clear: Teresa wanted me and, my god, did I want her.

After that we talked for another five minutes, though I cannot possibly remember what we talked about.

Suddenly, Teresa fixed me with those sexy, hazel eyes and jumped to the main topic. 'I think I want to share myself with you. Do you want to share yourself with me?' I'd never heard anyone describe sex that way, but it immediately seemed like the perfect approach to the subject. I nodded, as slowly and as ceremoniously as I could.

Within moments, Teresa had stood up, kimono still wide open, moved across the room and taken me by the hand. Without saying anything, just flashing a smile, she led me to another room. The door was closed, but I knew it wasn't the kitchen.

Then, right before we reached the room, she turned and asked me the weirdest question of the evening. 'Who's your favourite character from Greek mythology?'

'My favourite character … ?'

'Yes. Who do you really like? Or really identify with.'

Greek mythology? All I could think about was that bang-up movie with Eric Bana and Brad Pitt-Bull. I saw it three times, once on DVD when I was really drunk. 'Umm … I guess Hector. Or Achilles. One of those two. Depends on my mood really.'

She smiled. 'Yes, they're interesting too. Very manly.' She then tossed her longish, full hair around vigorously, like a banner. 'My favourite is Teiresias. Obviously.'

'Oh yeah, of course. That's what I would have guessed.' I had no idea at that point who the fuck Teiresias was. But it didn't really matter, because two seconds later, she took my head in her hands, pulled me towards her and started kissing me passionately.

Her tongue eased its way into my mouth, then started twisting slowly against my tongue. Then it started moving more intensely, desperately almost. It was as if there was something inside me, perhaps concealed, that Teresa needed to find, to recover and then take as much of that as she could before we broke our kiss.

As the kiss went on, I started feeling really strange. She slid her tongue out, grabbed the sides of my head—she was somewhat strong still—and looked me deep in the eyes.

'Don't resist. Just don't resist it. Let your feelings come through and swirl you in any direction they're moving. Be honest with your feelings. Please.' She then closed her eyes and we started kissing again. But even more intensely now. It was incredible.

She moved her hand down to the front of my pants and started rubbing. I was already standing tall and proud, as hard as I could possibly be. She stroked me expertly with a skilful palm. I imagined that she must have been a great masturbator back when she was still a guy.

Abruptly, she broke the kiss, put her mouth against my throat and whispered. 'Let's go inside. I can't wait any longer.'

'I can't wait any longer, too,' I replied—which was pretty obvious at that point.

Without turning from me, Teresa reached back and opened the door. She flipped on a low-glow light and stepped to the bed. The kimono slid to the floor. With her back still towards me, she raised her head and moved it gently. She also twisted her torso slightly as if to show off all the contours of her naked back and rump. She then arched one foot upwards to flaunt her shapely legs. I was pulling wildly at my clothes to get them off when she finally turned her head. 'Hurry with that. You want some help? I can't wait to feel you inside me.'

'No, I can handle it. I'm almost there.' I pulled my pants off roughly and tore off my underpants. She was now lying back on the bed, her left knee arched upwards, legs spread, eyes focused on the ceiling as if there was some message, some instructions there. Or some warning.

Finally naked, I climbed onto the bed, pulled myself against

Teresa's naked body and started kissing her. It was again that intense, deep penetration kiss. I had my right leg arched over her legs and she immediately started stroking it with her left hand. She then slowly ran her fingertips up the leg until she hit the fork in the road, applying just enough pressure with her nicely clipped nails to make it painfully sensuous.

I rolled back over slightly and started stroking her pussy, first with tightly drawn fingers, then with just two fingers stroking the gash. Then I slowly inserted the middle finger, making a circular motion as it moved deeper into her. She gave out a gasp. 'Oh god; that's so nice.' I twirled a little more and then, strangely, she grabbed my wrist sharply and pulled my hand away.

'I want to come with you inside me. Also, you shouldn't do that too long or it will go dry. See, I have to use a lubricant. Natural wetness is the one thing the operation couldn't provide.'

She then grabbed my sides gently and helped ease me onto her eager body. I suddenly spooked, like a young horse, and was afraid I might go soft. The finger was one thing, but here I was about to enter a woman who'd spent most of her life as a man. That was still bothering me somewhere deep inside.

But I was very close already, so Teresa eased me down, then took my rigid penis, pulled it against the lip of her vagina and twirled it around on the hair and the wet entrance, then started pulling me into her.

After she had taken in the crown of my cock, I did the rest, with a slow, easy push all the way in. Then I suddenly said to myself, 'This is it. You are inside a woman who nature had intended to be a man.' What might happen in here??

At first the pussy felt funny, like something that didn't belong there. I wanted to pull out, apologise, wipe myself off, apologise again, dress as quickly as I could and run out of there. But I knew I wouldn't. After a few strokes, I felt much more comfortable. And before long, it became very pleasurable. Teresa's vagina was very tight and though not as deep as I would have liked, it fitted me nicely.

In fact, I thought I was about to come after less than a minute; that's how good the pussy was. I closed my eyes and stiffened up my lower parts. Teresa slowed down her own stroking to a near halt. 'You almost came, didn't you?'

'Yes, but— '

'Don't worry, darling; that often happens. Most of the guys I've known, they lose control quickly with my vagina. So let's just relax, take it slow, and get used to the feel of the pussy.'

Which is exactly what I was trying to do. After another minute or so of soft thrust and pull, I felt more used to the sensation. Then we steadily picked up tempo and force, moving with an intensity I'd only known with a few women.

As we moved, Teresa started thrusting energetically. She suddenly called out, 'I love it, I love it. Oh, I really love it. You feel so right. This is what I want; you.'

'You're what I want too. You feel so right.' We were now going full throttle. Teresa's pumping under me was, not surprisingly, unique. It was as if she was trying to regain some lost and essential part of herself in the act of sex. Though I was trying to constrain myself as much as I could, I came more quickly than was usual for me. As she was still going, I kept pumping as long as I could, but finally, I slumped against her, thoroughly exhausted. I was sucking in short, shallow breaths and the air in the room had this wonderful sour taste to it.

For the next I'm-not-sure-how-many minutes we lay there, holding each other, mumbling words. I asked her if she enjoyed it, what it was like, if she came. She answered 'yes, definitely yes' to all three. I wanted details, but thought I should let the whole thing simmer for awhile before I started trawling for them.

About ten minutes later, we started kissing again, first just affectionately, then passionately. I was getting hard again after about thirty seconds of this. I started to climb aboard, but she pushed me back and said she had to go to the loo first, to urinate and then to re-lubricate. Before she climbed out of bed, she took my head in her hands and gave me a soft, very loving kiss. I may have been wrong because of the dim light, but I thought I detected a sadness in her face as she moved away.

As I waited for her to come back, I tended to the maintenance of my erection. I wanted to make sure it was ready for action upon her return, but that return was delayed ... and delayed. It wasn't too long, I suspect, before I slid into a deep sleep, probably a combination of the wine, the excitement and the exhaustion of our love-making.

I woke up in the early shafts of morning light, all alone in the bed. I hauled myself up to a sitting position and noted the slight headache pushing against my temples and forehead. I somehow found my shorts behind a chair, pulled them on and headed out to the living room.

Teresa was there on the long, plush couch, apparently asleep. She had a bath towel wrapped loosely around her waist, a long pink T-shirt pulled over her torso, and was wearing those sort of black blindfold things people wear on planes when they're trying to catch some sleep. I walked over to her quietly and touched her left shoulder lightly.

'Is that you?'

'Were you expecting anyone else?' She smiled at this.

'What time is it?'

'Early.'

'That must be why I'm still so tired.'

'May also have something to do with the exercise we managed to sneak in.'

'Maybe.' She took a deep sigh. 'So, Raymond ... or should I call you Hector?'

'Whatever suits you.'

'Was it everything you thought it would be?'

I didn't really know how to answer that, but rather than allowing myself to be choked by silence, I said it was even better than I ever thought. I then sucked back my lips before admitting, 'It was one of the most fantastic sexual experiences I've ever had.'

'Good. That's what I was hoping I could give you.'

I looked down at that beautiful face and thought I saw tears trickling down from just under the blindfold.

'Teresa, is there something wrong?'

'No, no; everything's just right. Look, there are a couple of things I have to do. I really have to do them before too late, and I need solitude to do them in. I don't mean to be brusque or impolite, but ...'

'No, no, of course. I understand. You've got things that have to be done.'

'Thank you.'

She sat up from the couch for the first time, pointed to the coffee table next to the couch and asked me to get her the pad of paper sitting there. I did. She tore the top sheet off and handed it to me. 'This is my phone number. Give me a call. I'll be sort of busy for the next few days, but I'll be very free after that.'

'Okay.'

She then slid back into her recumbent position on the couch. I grabbed the last of my things that were lying around and got ready to leave. Suddenly, she spoke again.

'Let me ask you: do you really have any idea who Teiresias was?'

I laughed. 'Not a clue.'

She gave a chugging laugh. 'Teiresias was this guy in Greek mythology who had a good position; a top assistant to one of the gods. Anyone, one day he was walking along, saw these two snakes copulating, thrashed them with his walking stick, and was turned into a woman as a "punishment".'

'Ooo.'

'Then, one day, Zeus and Hera—the king and queen of the gods?—they had this argument about who gets more pleasure in sex, a man or a woman. So they asked Teiresias, because she knew both sides. Teiresias was certain: woman have much more pleasure in sex.'

'I see. And would you agree with that?'

'Who am I to argue with my role model?' I laughed at that one.

We exchanged a few more rounds of banter, and then I had to go. She asked me to kiss her goodbye, which I did even though she remained lying on the couch with her blindfold on. I tried to lift it off for this last kiss, but she resisted strongly. 'I don't have to see you. I still see you, see you the way you were when we were one. That's the best view, believe me.' I relented.

I smoothened out the blindfold and leaned into her lightly. It was a warm and gentle kiss, one that promised future meetings.

But I never saw her again. For the next few days, I kept calling and getting a message to leave a message. I left about two dozen of them, some of the later ones rather angry or pitifully desperate. After the third day, when I called, I was told the number was no longer in operation.

I then drove out to where she lived. Because it was a condo, I couldn't get past the guards. I tried to explain that I needed to see Teresa, to clarify something, but these guys weren't very helpful. Well, to be fair, I wasn't even sure of her apartment number or the building she was in. I thought I knew, but the guards, of course, wouldn't let me go in and wander around to check.

I tried to describe her, but what could I say—that I was looking for a beautiful woman who used to be a man named David? I didn't even know her last name. For that matter, was Teresa itself her real name? Was there *anything* about this person that was one hundred percent real?

I went to the club were he had met, went quite a few times in fact, but she never came back. At least not on the evenings I was there. It was as if she'd just disappeared.

Well, she did warn me more than once that evening that she was complex. I guess I should always be grateful to her for letting me see that I myself was more complex than I'd ever imagined. In some ways, it was the most unforgettable night of my life. In other ways, it was a night I will probably spend the rest of my life trying to forget.

Alaric Leong is a proud Singaporean and aspiring author. Having worked as a PR writer, he decided to gravitate into a brand of fiction that hews a little more closely to reality. Another of his first attempts at fiction has been included in the anthology, *Crime Scene: Singapore* (Singapore: Monsoon Books, 2010).

Copyright Notices

BEST OF SINGAPORE EROTICA

LQ Pan & Richard Lord (Editors)

Now in its third edition, this wildly popular compendium of erotic writing from Singapore is as hot and steamy as the city-state itself. Absolutely nothing is out of bounds, offering readers a glimpse into the erotic lives of Singapore's inhabitants.

Gerrie Lim, author of bestselling *Invisible Trade*, reports on the island's hidden world of high-end escorts, Felix Cheong muses on exotic dancers and their customers and blogger Miss Izzy serves up some raunchy new fiction. Local luminaries Kirpal Singh and Robert Yeo weigh in with poetry and prose, and are joined by well-known Singapore writers O Thiam Chin, Jonathan Lim, Cyril Wong and Chris Mooney-Singh. The female voice is articulated in a variety of social settings by Samarah Zafirah, Meihan Boey, Alice Lee Am and Alison Lester.

'Singapore continues to shed its squeaky clean image. First there was Sexpo, then Crazy Horse. Now it's *Best of Singapore Erotica*, a collection of 27 pieces of short fiction and poems of a sensual and explicit nature'

The Straits Times, Singapore

ISBN: 978-981-05-5301-2

(www.monsoonbooks.com.sg/bookpage_0553012.html)